SINFUL SURRENDER

THE SINFUL SERIES
BOOK ONE

ERIKA WILDE

Copyright © Erika Wilde, June 2019
Print Edition

Cover Photo: Wander Aguiar Photography
Cover Design: Maria @ Steamy Designs
Editor: Amy Knupp, Blue Otter Editing
Developmental Editor: Dana with Danja Tales

All rights reserved. No part of this book may be used or reproduced in any manner whatsoever without permission except in the case of brief quotations embodied in critical articles and reviews. This book is a work of fiction. Names, characters, places and incidents are either products of the author's imagination or used fictitiously. Any resemblance to actual events, locals, or persons, living or dead, is entirely coincidental. All rights reserved. No part of this publication can be reproduced or transmitted in any form or by any means, electronic or mechanical, without permission in writing from the Author.

SINFUL SURRENDER

A debt repaid . . . in the form of her surrender.

Rich and powerful, Maddux Wilder has built his empire with one thought in mind . . . exacting revenge against the man who killed his parents. But he never planned for his enemy's daughter, Arabella Cole, to offer herself in exchange for her father's debt. Innocent and captivating, Maddux can't resist her allure, or the lust she stirs within him.

When Arabella sacrifices her life to save her father's, she does so with the intention of hating the man who now owns her. But beneath Maddux's gruff, boorish exterior she discovers a compelling man. One who makes her burn with need and awakens deep, forbidden desires she can't deny. Soon she's surrendering more than just her body to Maddux.

What starts as an act of vengeance becomes something far more consuming. Can this beauty tame the beast, or will revenge cost them both everything that matters most?

SINFUL SURRENDER is a seductive and modern take on Beauty and the Beast.

CHAPTER ONE

TONIGHT WAS THE night. After fourteen long years, Maddux Wilder was finally going to extract the revenge he'd been plotting and planning against the man responsible for his parents' deaths. Theodore Cole had no idea that he was about to become Maddux's bitch, which made his retribution all the sweeter.

Maddux smirked to himself as he tossed back a shot of bourbon while waiting for his sister and brother to meet him in his private penthouse office, located on the top floor of the five-story massive warehouse he'd renovated, modernized, and adapted into a functional, practical structure that he and his siblings lived in and shared. Each floor was specific in its design and purpose... from the ground level that was a common area and where tonight's charity ball would be held in the upscale ballroom, to the second floor where the three of them each had sectioned-off offices for business, to the third through fifth levels that were designated as living spaces.

His brother, Hunter, resided on the third floor, while his sister, Tempest, occupied the fourth, and since Maddux had funded the entire project, he'd laid claim to the top level of the building, which he'd transformed into a penthouse apartment that included a rooftop terrace and a three-hundred-sixty-degree view of the New York skyline.

Realtors had called him certifiably insane for purchasing the dilapidated building in the run-down warehouse district of Brooklyn when he easily could have purchased an entire city block of Fifth Avenue in Manhattan. But being one of those pretentious city boys had never been his style, and he'd instead invested in the immediate surrounding area so that he could gradually gentrify the neighborhood, which was already a work in progress.

He might have billions in the bank thanks to the success of MadX-Tech, but deep inside, he liked living close to where he'd grown up because it reminded him of his roots, where he'd come from, and most importantly, of his deceased immigrant parents who'd worked their asses off to provide for their family before their lives had been cut short. And living here kept him humble in the face of the obscene amount of money he'd accumulated in such a short amount of time.

But just because the outside of the warehouse looked weathered and he even had two men on payroll to clean up the trash and graffiti that appeared around the building on the daily until the entire neighborhood was renovated, that didn't mean he'd spared any expense *inside* the structure during the remodel. Including a state-of-the-art security system that ensured the only people who got into the building were actually invited inside. Including the men and women who would be arriving shortly for the ball. The only way past security was their name on tonight's guest list and proof of identification to confirm who they were.

He set his empty glass on a round, polished wooden table and poured himself a second shot of the dark amber liquid, finding it amusing that the crème de la crème of New York's society didn't hesitate to travel to Brooklyn to attend the opulent Wilder Way charity ball because it was always *the* event of the year. Anyone who was rich, powerful, or influential in any way wanted to be seen at the lavish affair, which was covered by the *New York Post's* Page Six.

Yes, the power that came with money and wealth was like an intoxicating drug that everyone wanted a hit of, but for Maddux, building his fortune had always been a means to an end. One fueled by the desire to destroy the man who'd so callously ripped Maddux's family apart. For years, he'd controlled his rage, had honed that fury into something more deliberate and precise, waiting for the right moment to present itself.

Now, retribution was so fucking close he could taste it.

"Starting your celebrating without us?" his

sister, Tempest, asked in that sweet, lilting voice of hers just as Maddux lifted his glass to his lips.

He swallowed the drink, watching as his stunning sister sashayed into the room with her normal dramatic flair that never failed to turn heads wherever she went, followed by their brother, Hunter, who was tugging at the collar of his white dress shirt, his expression darkened by an annoyed grimace.

"It's about damn time you two showed up," Maddux said, pouring them both a tumbler of the same bourbon he'd already indulged in, and topping his off in the process. Yeah, he sounded gruff and like an asshole, but these two siblings that he'd raised on his own meant everything to him. They were literally the only two people on the planet that he loved.

"Goddamn bow tie took me forever to get right and it still feels like it's choking me," Hunter muttered irritably as he gave Tempest a sidelong glance. "I fucking hate black-tie affairs and I'm only wearing this stupid tuxedo because I don't want to look like a bum off the streets in a pair of jeans and a T-shirt."

Tempest glided up to Hunter and pushed his hand away from his throat with a sigh, then did a little trick that loosened his brother's bow tie just enough to ease the grumpy look on his face because he could now breathe again.

His sister patted Hunter on his chest in a placating manner. "You know, if you had a woman around, she would have taken care of the bow tie situation for you like I just did," she said pointedly, always finding a way to remind both Maddux and Hunter that they needed to find a nice girl to settle down with.

As if that was ever going to fucking happen. Up to this point, there had been no single woman who'd interested him long enough to make a lifetime commitment to. Then again, he didn't date, and he specifically chose female companions for the sole purpose of fucking, and always picked ones who were agreeable to his kind of more depraved tendencies in the bedroom. Women were easily lured in by his dark good looks and the handsome, chiseled face he knew he'd been blessed with, but they were always, eventually, driven away by his brooding disposition, brusque attitude, and his lack of attention and affection.

They all thought they could tame the beast, but it would never happen because he had no room in his life for that softer, weaker emotion called love.

"As for *me* being a few minutes late," Tempest went on as she executed a theatrical twirl that made the skirt of her ball gown billow around her legs before she stopped and struck a regal pose, "*this* kind of magnificence takes time."

His sister *was* magnificent and strikingly beautiful. There was no disputing that claim. The formal dress she'd chosen for tonight's Wilder Way charity ball, the theme of which was fairy tales and happily ever afters—Tempest's idea, not his—was a deep scarlet red and very fitting to her personality and her fiery name. But as her older brother, Maddux couldn't help but scowl at the low neckline that displayed way too much cleavage and the amount of leg displayed by the front design of the dress.

"Jesus, Temp, could that slit in your dress get any higher?" he groused.

She batted her long black lashes at him. "Oh, dear brother, it most definitely could," she said in that sweet, patient tone she'd perfected just to use on him because she knew it irritated the shit out of him. "But I thought I'd leave a *little* bit to the imagination," she added with a saucy wink.

Hunter laughed. "That's surly Maddux speak for *you look gorgeous*, Tempest."

Her red, glossy lips curved into a soft, appreciative smile. "Thank you."

His brother's gaze swept over her pretty face, her lovely features made more prominent by the dark hair she'd swept back into some kind of intricate updo that was held together with random sparkling rhinestones and pearl pins. Maddux didn't miss the melancholy look that etched Hunter's expression, and he steeled himself for what he knew his sibling was going to say before he even spoke.

"You look so much like Mom," Hunter said to their baby sister, his voice rough with the kind of emotion they only visited on rare occasions, and tonight was definitely one of those. "She'd be so proud of the woman you are today."

Maddux felt his throat tighten and saw the sadness and glimmer of moisture gathering in his sister's eyes, which she valiantly held back as she gave them both a tremulous smile to dispel the too sentimental moment settling between all of them.

"And you two look extremely dashing in your tuxedos."

Maddux arched a brow. "Dashing?" he mocked the old-fashioned term. "Really?"

"Yes, *really*, Maddy," she said, right back to her sassy self while using the nickname she'd given him the first time she'd ever spoken his name as a toddler. "At least I'd never make the mistake of calling you Prince Charming."

She snorted at her own retort, and Hunter snickered in solidarity because that was the last label anyone would use to describe Maddux, who was more ruthless beast than the man of any woman's dreams.

"But for the sake of the theme of tonight's ball, dashing definitely fits." She gave her head a distinct nod that made the long, ruby earrings hanging from her lobes dance against her slender neck. "Fairy tales and happily ever afters," she reminded him.

Maddux refrained, just barely, from rolling his eyes as he handed Hunter one of the short glasses of bourbon, then Tempest the other, so they were all three holding a cut crystal tumbler. "By the way, you did an amazing job transforming the ballroom," he complimented his sister, who was solely responsible for coordinating the event's theme and selecting all the decor.

Out of curiosity, Maddux had taken a look a few hours earlier just to see the general setup of the lower level of the warehouse, and he'd been blown away by the transformation and details he'd encountered. As he'd walked into the ballroom, he'd literally felt as though he'd been transported into an enchanted land in a whole different world.

"This year's charity ball is going to be one for the books, that's for sure," Tempest said, exhaling a deep breath.

"In more ways than one," Hunter added, more serious now since all three of them were very aware of what was going to happen at some point this evening. For the Wilder siblings, tonight's event wasn't going to be all fun and games.

Maddux solemnly nodded in agreement. "Yes, it will be."

"He stole our parents from us and ruined our lives, Maddy," Tempest said in a strained whisper, her lower lip trembling ever so slightly. "Make him pay."

"I will," he promised, gently squeezing his sister's hand, even though a part of him knew that nothing would ever come close to making up for the cruel, brutal devastation that Theodore Cole had wreaked on their lives fourteen years ago. But Maddux was going to do everything in his power—of which he'd amassed plenty of over those long years of waiting and strategically planning—to make certain the man *wished* he were dead.

Hunter lifted his tumbler in the small, close circle they'd made around each other. "To Mom and Dad," he said, offering up the toast.

"To Mom and Dad," Maddux and Tempest both repeated wholeheartedly at the same time.

The sound of three glasses clinking simultaneously echoed through the office, then they each downed the fiery liquid fortitude.

The trap had been set, the wheels already in motion, and by the end of the night, Maddux would have Theodore Cole by the balls.

CHAPTER TWO

Arabella Cole couldn't remember the last time she'd been as excited about anything as she was about attending the exclusive, posh Wilder Way charity ball tonight. As she glanced out the tinted window of the limousine her father had rented for the evening and watched the inner city of Brooklyn pass them by, anticipation filled her until she was practically fidgeting in her seat.

She still couldn't believe that she was going to attend one of the biggest, most upscale benefits of the year. The one she'd always read about in the *New York Post's* Page Six the day after while dreaming wistfully of what it would be like to dress up in a gorgeous ball gown and pretend she was a princess for a night. So, after years of imagining herself at a Wilder Way charity benefit, she'd been shocked when she'd come across the gold-embossed invitation on her father's desk at home over a month ago when he'd never received one before.

She had no idea how he'd managed to score an invitation to the ball, but the theme of the event—fairy tales and happily ever afters—spoke to the romantic, fanciful girl inside her. The one who was still waiting for her own chivalrous Prince Charming to come along and sweep her off of her feet.

It had been in that moment as she'd touched the gold lettering that Arabella finally knew exactly what she wanted for her twenty-fifth birthday, which her father had been asking about. She didn't want more jewelry or designer purses or outrageously expensive and impractical gifts that she'd never use. Her father would have found a way to give her the moon and stars if she'd ever asked for them, and while she knew she was incredibly fortunate to have a parent who doted on her, it wasn't tangible, extravagant things she wanted in her life.

No, she wanted more independence and the kind of free rein that didn't include checking in with her father on a regular basis so he was aware of her whereabouts all the time. But she had to admit that a part of her felt guilty for those selfish thoughts because her dad had always been so good to her and she worried about him, too, since he'd recently been diagnosed with angina, a symptom of coronary heart disease. While he was currently stable, she knew any upset could possibly trigger an episode.

Arabella had been so sheltered and protected growing up after her mother passed away, and she was itching to explore the world on a grander scale instead of existing in the padded bubble her father had created around her. She knew her father would never grant that kind of request—he was too protective for that—so she asked for the one thing she'd always desired. She'd asked to go to the ball.

And she swore tonight would be the beginning of a new, adventurous side to Arabella Cole. How could a theme like fairy tales and happily ever afters be anything but a magical, enchanting experience?

Unfortunately, the one thing putting a major damper on the evening was the man sitting beside her, Gavin Scott, who'd been her father's right-hand man in business for years and who Theodore Cole had insisted accompany her to the ball. That had been the one caveat to her dad granting her request, and because her father had been oddly reluctant about allowing her to attend the ball in the first place, she'd agreed to his stipulation, even knowing it was her father's way of forcing Arabella to acknowledge Gavin's interest in her.

She tried not to let that thought ruin her excitement. Her dad had already tried the gentle nudging method to push her toward Gavin romantically, and while she'd given in to a few dates with the man, there had been no spark between them for her, even when she'd kissed him. What turned her off the most was that he was too conceited, too aggressive, and too egotistical for her taste . . . not that her disinterest dissuaded him in any way. It was as though he took her cool, aloof disposition toward him as a challenge, instead of accepting that she disliked him despite her father's attempts at matchmaking.

Gavin was undeniably good-looking, with sandy-blond hair and green eyes, but that outward appearance didn't make up for his narcissistic tendencies, along with the fact that he already acted as though Arabella belonged to him. That in itself irritated her immensely because she was *not* his property. But for tonight, for the sake of being civil and enjoying her evening, she'd smile and pretend that she wasn't coming to despise Gavin and his unpleasant personality, the too familiar way he touched her, and his overbearingly possessive ways.

Still gazing out the window, she shook off those troublesome thoughts so they didn't ruin her good mood, but she knew at some point she would need to address the situation with her dad and tell him exactly how she felt about Gavin. It wouldn't be an easy conversation since her father considered Gavin very much like the son he'd never had and had high hopes of them being the perfect couple.

In the limousine, her father and Gavin spoke in hushed tones, and for the most part, she'd shut out their conversation, as she normally did when she was in their presence, because it usually pertained to business she had no inkling about or interest in. But it was a comment that her father made beneath his breath that caught her attention. She listened a bit more intently while she continued to pretend as though she was riveted by the passing scenery.

"After all these years, I still have no idea how I ended up on the invite list for tonight's ball," he muttered, sounding oddly uneasy, which wasn't a word Arabella would ever use to describe her normally confident and direct father.

"It doesn't matter, Theo," Gavin replied arrogantly from his seat beside her. "Someone probably dropped your name to whoever is coordinating the event, and nobody higher up noticed the . . . mistake," he said, as if choosing his words carefully because Arabella was with them. "Consider it our good fortune, because there are connections to be made at the ball tonight that we wouldn't otherwise have access to."

"It better be worth it," her father grumbled. "It cost me a goddamn fortune to attend this asinine fairy-tale ball."

"Just keep your distance from Wilder, which should be easy enough to do, and everything will be fine," Gavin assured him. "Besides, he's not going to do anything that will make a scene in front of over three hundred people."

"Yes, you're probably right," her dad agreed with a sigh.

Arabella couldn't ignore that last part of the

conversation considering Gavin had pretty much indicated something bad could happen to her father if he crossed Wilder, not to mention they'd possibly been invited to the affair by mistake. She finally turned her head and glanced across the back of the limo, to the long leather seat where her father sat opposite of her and Gavin.

Her concern increased when she saw the dark frown on her dad's face, and she finally spoke. "Is there a reason you shouldn't have been invited to tonight's event, Father?"

Her dad's startled gaze snapped to hers. "What?" Her question seemed to make him irritable, and she watched as he managed to shake off his initial agitation while waving a dismissive hand in the air. "No . . . no, of course not."

It wasn't often that she didn't believe something her father told her, but this was one of the few times she had doubts, which was why she persisted. "Then why are you worried about someone making a scene?"

"It's a business-related issue, Ari," Gavin cut in, his tone as condescending as the way he patted her hand as if she were a child. "It's nothing you need to worry your pretty little head about. You just enjoy the ball and let us men handle things that don't concern you."

Her jaw clenched in annoyance and she sent Gavin a cutting glare, even though she knew it wasn't a flattering look for her. God, he was such a jerk, and she deliberately yanked her hand from under the heavy weight of his, hating the way he treated her as though she was stupid and had nothing but cotton candy for brains.

While she'd started the evening with an abundance of excitement, she couldn't deny that something suddenly felt off, despite her father's reassurances. The fact that Gavin had just suggested that there were possible business concerns that might crop up tonight certainly didn't relieve her worry.

She couldn't imagine what kind of contentious situation her father might be involved in. For as long as she'd been alive, he'd worked for Addingwell Financial as a partner, and he'd taken on Gavin as his associate about fourteen years ago, but other than those few details, he'd never shared the technicalities of his job. Her father always kept his business separate from the time he spent with her, and when she'd once asked him why he never talked about his work, he told her he liked to keep his focus on her and their relationship when he was home.

It was an easy enough excuse to believe, even if his vague response did increase her curiosity of what, exactly, her father did in finance. Clearly, it was something that made him a lot of money, because they lived a very comfortable life and cash never seemed to be an issue for anything he wanted to purchase for himself or her.

Her father glanced out his own window and grumbled beneath his breath again. The last two words she heard were Maddux Wilder, and the name was spoken with unmistakable disdain. This time, she kept her mouth shut and didn't ask questions because she knew Gavin would jump in with another insulting reply, and she was honestly afraid that she'd do something incredibly impulsive and unladylike—like tell him to go screw himself.

So she remained quiet, her hands clasped tightly in her lap on top of the gorgeous champagne-colored tulle and beading that made up her ball gown. She'd heard the name Maddux Wilder before tonight, usually in conjunction with the yearly ball, but there had been a few times when she'd overheard her father mention the other man's name in conversation with Gavin, but she'd never given another thought about it.

The limousine slowed behind a line of vehicles as they neared what looked to be an older warehouse, pulling Arabella from her thoughts. When they reached the surprisingly ordinary-looking building located in a low-income neighborhood, their driver was directed toward the underground parking structure by the security detail surrounding the place.

"Jesus," Gavin said, the one word dripping with disgust and ridicule. "Just look at this place."

His crass, obnoxious tone piqued Arabella's irritation and she narrowed her gaze his way. She couldn't deny that she'd conjured images of arriving at an opulent mansion outside the city limits for tonight's festivities, but she wasn't about to make any judgments until she *arrived* at the ball. From pictures she'd seen of past events, the interior of wherever the event was held was always lavish and extravagant.

"No need to be rude," she snapped at him, hating his sanctimonious attitude. "In case you didn't notice, the nearby neighborhoods we drove by are clearly being rehabilitated and modernized to revitalize this district."

The corners of Gavin's mouth curled into a patronizing smile. "You've always seen the world through rose-colored glasses, Ari. Trust me, no matter what renovations take place, this part of the city has been and always will be unworthy of the more elite people of the world."

"That's enough, Gavin," her father said in a surprisingly stern voice in an attempt to smooth things over between them. "How about the two of you put your differences aside and enjoy the evening?"

She gave him a sweet smile. "I plan to, Father." She wasn't going to let Gavin taint anything about this special, magical night for her. Which meant ditching him as quickly as an opportunity presented itself.

The limo finally came to a stop, and a valet dressed in a tuxedo opened her passenger door. He held out a hand to help Arabella and her huge, voluptuous dress out of the vehicle, followed by her father and Gavin. A few steps later, they had to verify their credentials with security before they were escorted along the long length of red carpet that led into the building.

Inside, the transformation was immediate and spectacular, causing Arabella to gasp as she took in the stunning, enchanting decor that had altered what was probably a normal and plain open common area when it wasn't in use for the yearly charity event. She'd barely begun to appreciate her surroundings when Gavin grabbed her by the elbow, pinching just hard enough to make her wince.

"Pay attention, Arabella," he said impatiently as he led her toward a group of guests where her father was already conversing with a few of the men. "Your head is always in the clouds and I don't want us to get separated or you getting lost in this huge crowd of people."

Was he for real? She rolled her eyes over his idiotic comment. Unfortunately, the mocking gesture was lost on him since he was looking straight ahead. "I'm a grown, twenty-five-year-old woman, Gavin," she reminded him, twisting her arm just enough that he was forced to let her go, and judging by the clench of his jaw, he didn't like that act of rebellion. "Not a three-year-old who needs a babysitter. Besides, do you not see the security in this place? Nothing is going to happen to me if I decide to take a look around on my own."

He gave her a dark stare that was just shy of

threatening. "You're my date," he said in a tone that brooked no argument. "I want you by my side tonight."

It was an unmistakable order, and his possessive behavior made anger and resentment bubble inside her, which was *not* how she intended to spend this amazing, once-in-a-lifetime kind of night. Since they were surrounded by a dozen other guests, she tamped down her temper the best she could for now because it was not the time or place to make a scene and set Gavin straight on the fact that he did not dictate to her or the decisions she made.

The men continued talking, clearly all very well acquainted. The women standing next to their husbands or dates were dressed in the most beautiful, extravagant gowns and dripping in glittering jewels. They looked stunning . . . and as bored as Arabella felt listening to business-related discussions.

Not in the mood to stand around and strike up social niceties with the ladies, she made sure that Gavin was engrossed in the male conversation before gradually inching away from him and toward the freedom to explore and experience this evening on her own terms. Eventually, she turned around and blended right into the throng of other guests, a veritable sea of silk and satin and black tuxedos.

Exhilaration swirled inside her as she accepted a glass of champagne from a waiter passing by with a silver tray of flutes. The first sip of the expensive bubbly wine was sweet on her tongue and tickled her throat on the way down. The second drink was just as smooth and decadent.

Without Gavin controlling her every move, she strolled around the ballroom, taking in everything around her with wide-eyed awe. The color scheme was soft pink and cream—from the opulent floral arrangements on the dinner tables and displayed on dozens of pedestals, to the gossamer fabric draping columns and the walls, to the dramatic up-lighting that created an elegant, romantic ambience to the room. She walked through an area that looked and felt like an enchanted forest with real, eight-foot trees wrapped in tulle and twinkling lights, feeling as though she'd entered an enchanted wonderland. Candles floated in a huge marble fountain, and the crystal chandeliers overhead cast stunning prisms of light everywhere.

She passed by a sweeping staircase that led to a second-story balcony that overlooked the ballroom, and she would have explored that upper floor, too, except for the red velvet rope securing the area as off-limits to guests. So, she moved on to the silent auction to peruse the items just for fun and found herself tempted to put a bid on a rare collection of first-edition Jane Austen novels. She took a chance and jotted down an offer that was more than her monthly salary, though she had the amount in her savings to cover the cost if she was lucky enough to win. But as soon as she heard a familiar voice starting to sing around another corner where she'd seen an elaborately decorated stage earlier, she quickly headed in that direction . . . trading in her now empty champagne glass for a full one on the way, excited to see tonight's entertainment perform live and in person.

Raevynn Walsh was one of the hottest pop stars climbing the charts over the past few years, rivaling Taylor Swift's kind of success. She wrote her own songs and had the kind of unique and stirring voice that drew in listeners—airy and angelic when she sang ballads and throaty and raw when she belted out her rock tunes. Right now she was singing her current number one hit, "You Don't Know Me," while working the stage and entertaining the audience with fast-paced choreographed moves that kept everyone engaged.

She was remarkably gorgeous, with long, wavy blonde hair that fell halfway down her back, and wearing a skintight, black sparkling mini-dress with stiletto heels. When she finished that bold, sexy performance, the lights on the stage dimmed while she disappeared behind a partition with her name emblazoned on it for an outfit change. A wooden swing, decorated in vines and flowers, gradually descended from the ceiling. By the time the prop was all the way down, Raevynn returned, this time wearing a flowing, crystal-studded lilac ball gown that made her look like a regal princess.

She sat down on the swing, and as it began to slowly sway back and forth across the stage, the melody to Arabella's favorite ballad, "Wishing for You," began to play. The lights dimmed even more as Raevynn began to sing the heartfelt lyrics, about longing for that one person who could see beyond the facade of her life and love her unconditionally.

Arabella might not know what it was like to be in the public eye all the time like Raevynn, but she understood the desire to find a man who accepted her for who and what she was, without trying to suppress the independent, free-spirited woman she craved to be.

Unfortunately, Arabella knew that as long as Gavin was a part of her life, and her father saw him as the perfect suitor for his daughter, she'd have to fight damn hard for her own wishes, dreams, and happily ever after.

CHAPTER THREE

MADDUX STOOD IN the shadows of the private second-story balcony that overlooked the charity ball below, the perfect spot for him to watch Theo's and Gavin's every move before deciding it was time to confront the unscrupulous man Maddux had spent the past fourteen years despising.

He'd been aware of the two men since the moment they'd arrived thanks to his security team, who'd immediately alerted him to their presence—along with Theo's beautiful daughter, Arabella. She'd only taken a few steps into the ballroom when she'd come to a sudden stop, her lips parting and her eyes growing wide in wonder, seemingly mesmerized by the impressive layout and striking, elegant decor that greeted her.

The joyful pleasure that transformed her pretty features riveted Maddux more than it should have, as did the way her champagne-colored dress fitted so precisely to her midsection, much like a corset. The cinched-in fabric started just above her hips and molded to the indentation of her tiny waist that he was certain he'd be able to span very easily with his large hands. The snug bodice pushed up the creamy swells of her small breasts, and the fluttery sleeves of her gown draped gracefully halfway down her slim arms, leaving her shoulders and neckline bare, except for the soft, rich brown curls that fell strategically from the rest of the hair that was knotted loosely at the nape of her neck.

Since he'd employed a private investigator whose sole purpose was to report to him weekly on anything relating to Theodore Cole, which included the other man's relationship with his daughter, Maddux had been privy to dozens of pictures of Arabella over the years—most from faraway or blurred, zoomed-in shots—but the reality of seeing all that natural beauty up close didn't compare to those random photos.

He'd also been apprised of her life in general in those weekly reports, and as much as he'd wanted his PI to unearth some kind of deceitful information on Arabella Cole so he could hate her as much as he did her father, it quickly became clear to Maddux that Theo had gone to great lengths to shelter and protect his precious daughter from the harsh realities of what he *really* did for a living.

He knew Arabella's mother had died when she'd been a child, and from there she'd been raised by nannies until she'd been old enough to attend a private, all-girls boarding school in Connecticut, which had given Theo the freedom to conduct his business dealings without his daughter underfoot. The same living arrangements had applied to college, where she'd earned her degree in English literature and then gone on to attain her master's in library science.

For the past few years, she'd been living with her father in the city while working at a private university library as a digital data analyst and curator—a fancy description for someone who collected, preserved, and archived digital assets and resources. Clearly, she was intelligent and probably a little nerdy considering her profession.

Maddux even had a file on the men she'd dated, which was woefully slim. She didn't have any history of a long-term relationship with any man, and Maddux was certain that had everything to do with Gavin, Theodore's right-hand man, who wanted Arabella for himself. It was also documented in a few of the reports Maddux had received from his PI that, whenever she went out on a date with someone new, things between her and the guy always abruptly ended. Unbeknownst to Arabella, Gavin had warned those suitors to back off, and there must have been an implied threat in his request, because every single one immediately complied.

Maddux shook his head in disgust. God, it truly amazed him that a man so evil and corrupt as Theodore Cole could have produced a daughter so lovely and sweet and guileless . . . and completely naive to her father's, and Gavin's, dirty dealings.

Gavin, now seemingly impatient with Arabella's excitement and fascination with the ball's decor, grabbed her arm, rough enough to make her wince in discomfort as he jerked her in the direction her father had walked off toward and said something to her that was accompanied with a harsh narrowing of his gaze.

Fucking asshole, Maddux thought irritably . . . then felt the corner of his mouth twitch with rare amusement when he caught Arabella rolling her eyes behind Gavin's back before she wrenched her arm from his grasp in an act of defiance. An argument of some sort ensued between them, and it was obvious to Maddux even from this distance that Arabella wasn't taking whatever shit Gavin was dishing out.

Despite her petite size, she clearly had a backbone and wasn't a shrinking violet. She did follow him to a group of guests where her father was conversing with a few of the men, but it didn't take her long to slip away and blatantly defy Gavin a second time once he no longer paid attention to her.

Knowing his security detail was focused on Theodore until Maddux summoned for him later this evening, Maddux switched his attention to Arabella as she explored the connecting areas downstairs, her delight and exhilaration restored now that she was alone again. Her gown billowed around her as she walked, giving the impression she was floating across the imported marble floor. She took in *everything* around her while enjoying first one, then a second glass of champagne.

While he didn't usually give women more than a passing glance unless he was looking for an easy lay, this one—his sworn enemy's daughter—inexplicably intrigued him . . . more than he cared to admit, considering who her father was and what Theodore had done to Maddux's parents.

As he watched her stop at the stage where Raevynn Walsh, the evening's entertainment, was singing, Maddux decided that he was going to do something that was completely unscripted. He was going to make a bold and very unforgettable statement to Theodore and Gavin that *nothing* was off-limits when it came to this new and menacing game they were about to play, where Maddux was now the one in control.

He was going to put his hands on the sweet, beautiful, unassuming Arabella and leave his mark, even if only subtly, he decided as he headed down the private stairway to the lower level. He was going to prove to Theodore that *he* now had the ability to hurt the other man where he'd feel it the most—his daughter. It was only a matter of time before Gavin went searching for Arabella, and when he found her, Maddux had no doubt that the man would *not* be pleased with what he discovered.

Maddux was fucking counting on it.

Raevynn switched to a softer, slower melody

as he came to a stop a few deliberate inches behind Arabella, who had her hands clasped beneath her chin and was swaying gently back and forth, oblivious to everything but the woman performing on the stage.

He could hear Arabella softly singing the lyrics, her own voice surprisingly melodious. Boldly, he settled his hand on the curve of her waist, gleaning her attention, just as he'd intended. She gasped at the too intimate touch and spun around, eyes initially narrowed because she'd clearly expected to see someone else. With her petite height, her gaze was level with his broad chest, and she slowly, gradually, tipped her head back to look up at his face.

The initial tension in her body eased, and she blinked at him in surprise, her features softening with unmistakable awareness. Shockingly, he felt the unwanted attraction, too.

"I'm sorry to startle you," he said with a deliberately charming grin meant to persuade her that he was a decent guy, even though his motives were less than pure. "But I thought maybe you'd like to dance?" He indicated the other couples gathering out on the nearby dance floor.

Her wide blue eyes filled with delight at the request, and the guileless smile that curved her perfect lips made his mind travel down a very sinful path filled with an inappropriate amount of lust.

She nodded, much more demurely than any

woman he'd ever dealt with. "Yes, I'd love to dance with you," she said, her voice sounding breathless, and even that eager response made his traitorous dick twitch.

He held out his hand, and she immediately placed her soft, slender fingers against his palm, automatically trusting him when he was the last person she ought to put her faith in. He led her out to the designated area in front of the stage and pulled her into his arms. Tentatively, she placed one of her hands lightly on his shoulder, but he wasn't so timid. Instead, he splayed a hand against her lower back and drew her flush against his body, much too aware of how small and delicate she was in comparison to his much larger, more muscular frame.

He wasn't much of a dancer, but he managed to sway in time to the slow song Raevynn Walsh was crooning.

"What is your name?" he asked, absently skimming his thumb along the back of the hand he was holding in his free one. It was an unnecessary question since he knew everything about her, but she didn't know that.

"Arabella."

He raised a brow. "Bella for short?"

"No." She licked her bottom lip a bit shyly and shook her head. "Actually, some call me Ari for short."

He produced another lighthearted smile, which felt much too foreign on his lips. "Bella is much more befitting considering how beautiful you are." It wasn't a lie. Arabella's features were stunning, her complexion like fine porcelain he wanted to touch and caress.

He caught the faint blush coloring her cheeks right before she ducked her head. "Thank you."

Clearly, she wasn't used to compliments from men and he found her modest reaction refreshing compared to the cunning women he normally dated. "Are you enjoying the ball?" he asked conversationally.

Her head popped back up, her features lighting up with excitement. "I just arrived a little bit ago, but yes, I'm enjoying it very much. It's my first time attending and it's everything I thought it would be and more. I'm a bit of a romantic, so the whole fairy-tale theme is so much fun."

As he listened to her ramble on and watched her animated expression, he forgot for a moment that he was dancing with his enemy's daughter. This was a woman he ought to feel nothing but disdain for, just due to her direct bloodline, but the shocking truth hit him hard.

He wanted Arabella Cole. He wanted to kiss those lush pink lips and sink his tongue deep inside her mouth to see just how sweet she tasted. The creamy swells of her breasts tempted him to bend his head and lick and bite that soft, plump flesh, and Jesus fucking Christ, images of having her naked and spread out on his huge bed, moaning his name as he drove deep inside her tight body, were invading his mind at rapid speed.

What the hell was the matter with him? He clenched his jaw, trying to steel himself from her irresistible allure... but she was looking up at him with those big blue eyes as though she was already halfway smitten with him. Fuck. All her seductive innocence was no match for the angry, jaded animosity he harbored deep in his soul for one man in particular... her father, who he had every intention of destroying.

And once Arabella discovered who Maddux truly was, and what he'd done to tear *her* family apart, that desire in her gaze would quickly and undoubtedly turn to hatred.

CHAPTER FOUR

ARABELLA FELT AS though she was being swept off her feet by the handsome, enigmatic man who'd asked her to dance, and it was a unique sensation that made her feel wonderfully light-headed and as though a dozen butterflies were fluttering around in her stomach.

After she'd gushed about attending the ball for the first time, an easy silence fell between them as Raevynn continued singing her ballad, and Arabella realized that while this man knew *her* name, she didn't know his. And since she'd like to believe that maybe they'd spend more time together this evening beyond this one dance, she ventured to find out.

She glanced up at his face—God, he was so big and tall she had to tip her head back to see that far up—and found him looking down at her with a heat and intensity in his amber eyes that made a shivery warmth trickle through her veins. She should have felt intimidated by his immense stature, by the slight tension in his jaw and the fact that his body was nearly twice as big as hers. His strong, muscled arms could effortlessly crush her if he so wished, but despite his commanding presence, she felt strangely safe and secure with him.

There was a certain edge about him that fascinated her. Though he wore a fitted tuxedo that had to have been tailor-made for his size, he looked nothing like most of the clean-cut men in attendance. His shaggy brown hair was long enough to fall rebelliously past the collar of his suit jacket and was finger combed away from the sharp, attractive angles of his face and jaw. She caught sight of what appeared to be a puckered scar along the side of his neck that disappeared into the collar of his shirt just where her hand rested on his shoulder, and she had to fight the urge to skim her fingers over that disfigured flesh and ask him what had happened.

"What is *your* name?" she asked when she could finally get her brain to engage properly without ogling him.

He hesitated a few noticeable seconds before answering. "Maddux Wilder."

Her lips parted in surprise. "*The* Maddux Wilder?"

The corner of his mouth quirked with what appeared to be amusement, and it was enough to soften the harsher lines of his face. "As far as I know."

Falling head over instant infatuation with the host of tonight's ball was the last thing Arabella ever expected to happen when she'd arrived this evening. But she couldn't deny her attraction to this man whose hand was pressed so intimately, possessively even, against the small of her back.

He tipped his head to the side curiously, though his gaze was direct and back to being intense. "How do you know of me?"

She flashed him a cheeky grin as he swept her in a slow circle in time to the music, causing his thigh to press ever so slightly between hers, yet firm enough to make her breath catch in her throat because of how arousing it felt. "Well, your name is directly connected to the charity ball, so there *is* that."

He chuckled, the sound low and deep . . . and somehow oddly relieved. "Ahhh, that's very true."

Seemingly catching something, or someone, in his peripheral vision, Maddux shifted his gaze from her face to over her shoulder. His entire body suddenly stiffened against hers, and a muscle in his cheek ticked as he clenched his jaw. His gaze flashed with animosity before he deliberately subdued the emotion, just as a hand clasped tight around Arabella's arm from behind her and tried pulling her away from Maddux.

Momentarily confused by what was happening, she clung tighter to Maddux, except the fingers around her upper arm held firm, pinching against her skin in a way that she immediately knew it was Gavin tugging at her, even before she turned her head to look at him.

His expression was furious, his voice dripping

with reproach as he berated her. "Didn't I tell you to stay close and not to wander off?"

She opened her mouth to issue the scathing response she'd been holding back since the limo ride, but Maddux spoke first.

"I would advise you to take your hands off her, Gavin," he said, his words a low, deliberate command and laced with unmistakable warning. "Now."

Gavin sneered at Maddux, making it clear that the two men knew one another on some level, and defiantly cinched his fingers tighter, causing a soft whimper of pain to escape Arabella's lips.

"I can put my hands anywhere I want on her," Gavin shot back daringly, openly defying Maddux's order. "This woman is *my* date for the evening."

A frightening rage flashed across Maddux's expression, and lightning quick, his hand shot out and clamped around Gavin's wrist. A battle of wills ensued as Maddux exerted enough pressure and strength that Gavin was forced to release her arm or risk his bones shattering under the increasing tenacity of Maddux's unrelenting grip.

As soon as Gavin finally, begrudgingly let her go, Maddux stepped back from Arabella but pinned Gavin with a hard, ruthless stare. "If this woman is your date for the evening, then maybe you ought to pay more attention to her or some other man is going to steal her right out from under you."

With Raevynn having finished her predinner set of songs, people had now started to glance their way, and much to Arabella's relief, Gavin came to his senses and realized that they were close to making a scene at a private venue. Whatever nasty reply he'd wanted to issue in response he wisely held back, but there was no mistaking the resentment seething off of Gavin.

Maddux turned back to her, the anger he'd just displayed with Gavin replaced by a surprising warmth and kindness as he picked up her hand, lifted it to his lips, and placed a gallant kiss on the backs of her fingers that made her heart flutter fancifully in her chest.

"It was a pleasure meeting and dancing with you, Bella," he said, his smooth, deep voice sounding genuinely gratified. "I hope you enjoy the rest of your evening."

With that, he turned around and walked away, blending into the crowd until Arabella could no longer see him.

"Fucking asshole," Gavin said, bitterness coating his derogatory words.

"Don't vilify him, Gavin," Arabella said, giving the other man a look filled with nothing but scorn and contempt, which was exactly how she felt about him and the situation. "Maddux was a gentleman for defending me, while you're the one who put a handprint on my arm that will most likely bruise by tomorrow because you felt you had the right to claim me like some caveman. But here's a news flash for you. You don't have *any* right to me at all."

Gavin's lips thinned with spite. "You have no idea who or what you're dealing with when it comes to Maddux Wilder. I'm warning you, Arabella. Stay away from him. He's a dangerous, malicious man."

The only dangerous, malicious man Arabella could see at the moment was Gavin, though she couldn't stop thinking about the conversation she'd overheard in the limousine on the ride over between him and her father, and the insinuation that something bad could possibly happen to her dad at tonight's ball.

Clearly, there was more between Maddux, her father, and Gavin than she knew about, but the man she'd just danced with had been nothing but respectful and considerate with her. More than Gavin had ever been. She wasn't sure what to make of any of it.

The serving of dinner was announced, and having remembered their assigned table from the invitation, Arabella started toward the dining area with Gavin beside her. As soon as she felt his attempt to touch her elbow to try and escort her, she wrenched her arm away, stopped in her tracks, and glared at him.

"Under any circumstance, do *not* touch me."

Annoyance flashed across his features at her blunt order, and for a moment, she thought he was going to do it anyway. Instead, his gaze darted around the near vicinity, and as if fearing that Maddux might appear to rip his hands off her again, he instead balled his fingers into fists at his sides.

"Stop being so childish," he snapped.

"I will when you stop being an overbearing *jerk*." She continued on to their table, leaving him to follow her like a pet dog.

Her father was already there, and when Gavin attempted to redeem himself by pulling out a chair for her, Arabella ignored the gesture and took the seat on the opposite side of her father, so that her dad was sitting between her and Gavin as a barrier.

Her father glanced at each one of them and sighed. "Did the two of you have another tiff?"

Arabella arranged the skirt of her dress beneath the table while smiling at her dad. "Yes, but I believe we've come to an understanding, and as long as Gavin keeps his hands off me for the foreseeable future, we'll be just fine, Father."

Her dad frowned at that announcement, and when he glanced at Gavin, the annoyed-looking man sitting beside him just shook his head as if to say he didn't want to talk about it, and Arabella was fine with that.

As the table around them filled up, Arabella conversed with the younger woman sitting beside her who was there with her parents, while they were treated to a five-course meal that had been prepared by a world-renowned Michelin star chef.

Everything was decadent and divine, and when the feast was over, she and her tablemate, Andrea, had become fast friends and decided to enjoy the rest of the evening in each other's company, instead of hanging out with their parents ... or Gavin.

As they explored the ballroom and all it had to offer, they drank champagne, ate chocolate-covered strawberries, and danced to the songs Raevynn belted out. She returned to the silent auction, bummed to see that the bidding on the Jane Austen novels had reached over one hundred grand, but Andrea cheered her up by dragging her over to the photo op area, where they took fun pictures with dramatic backdrops and silly, life-size cardboard cutouts of their favorite fairy-tale characters ... and with Arabella's earlier encounter with Maddux Wilder still on her mind, she chose the Beast image to pose with, since it reminded her so much of the rough-around-the-edges man who'd been surprisingly gentle with her yet tough enough to protect her from Gavin's abuse.

The next few hours passed quickly, and no matter where she and Andrea ended up, Arabella was on the constant lookout for Maddux, hoping to get another glimpse of him ... or dance with him again. Much to her disappointment, the host of the ball was nowhere to be seen.

After her fourth glass of champagne in as many hours, Arabella let Andrea know that she was headed to the ladies' room while her new friend, who was flirting with a man she'd just met, stayed behind. Ten minutes later, as she exited the women's lounge, she saw her father and Gavin walk by, being escorted toward the private stairs that led to the second-story balcony by a man she didn't recognize. Her father looked annoyed and reluctant as he followed the gentleman, who appeared to be in his late thirties, her dad's reddening face lined with enough anxiety to concern her.

She fell into step behind the three men, keeping to the columns and outer areas as she followed . . . close enough to hear their conversation and keep an eye on her father, but managing to stay out of their line of sight at the same time.

"Vincent, I don't think this is the time or place to address this matter," her dad said, his voice gruff with growing agitation.

The man named Vincent stopped at the staircase and turned to face her father, his dark gaze as shrewd as his expression as he addressed her dad. "You've avoided me and the situation for the past month, which is far more time than I allow any of my other borrowers," he said in a direct manner. "If this is my only way to get your attention and discuss repayment of your loan that is increasing by the day with interest fees, then so be it. You know exactly how this process works, so let's avoid the inevitable, shall we?"

As Arabella listened to the man's words, her

stomach twisted into painful knots at the notion that her father was in some kind of financial trouble. And from the sounds of things, he didn't owe money to a reputable institution, but rather someone who was quickly running out of patience with her father's inability to pay back the loan.

"I've dealt with your father since you were in diapers," her dad tried to reason, a slight desperation threading his voice. "He's never had a problem with me requesting a grace period or skipping a payment or two when things are tight."

"As you well know, my father is no longer running the business. *I* am, and I've been more than lenient with you and your many lapses in payment."

All business, Vincent unlatched the red rope securing the staircase and glanced from Gavin, who was still standing by her father's side, back to her dad. "Would you like to discuss this issue with or without Gavin in the room?"

Her father exhaled a breath, his complexion having paled considerably over the past few minutes. "He's aware of the situation and I would prefer that he be present."

A patronizing smirk curved the other man's lips. "We won't be breaking any bones today, if that's your concern."

"It's not," her father replied, but considering the nerves Arabella detected in his normally confident voice, she knew he was putting on a brave face.

With her heart beating wildly in her throat, she watched the trio ascend their way to the second level. Each step her father took was slow and tentative, as if he was about to face the gallows or something equally dreadful. When they rounded a corner and Arabella could no longer see them, she panicked because all she could think about was her father's weak heart and the possibility that this stressful situation might prompt another life-threatening attack.

Without hesitating, she advanced up the stairs as well, arriving on the balcony level just as the three men headed into a nearby room and the door closed behind them. Trying to keep the rustling of her skirts to a minimum, she quietly made her way to where they'd disappeared and did the only thing she could do without making her presence known . . . she pressed her ear to the door to hear the conversation on the other side and to find out what horrible fate awaited her father.

CHAPTER FIVE

THE FEAR THAT Maddux witnessed on Theodore's face the second the man realized he was trapped in a room with his greatest adversary was one of the most gratifying moments of Maddux's adult life. This moment of reckoning was fourteen long years in the making, and he was going to enjoy every fucking minute of it.

He planned to savor Theodore's panic and despair. The same panic and despair his parents undoubtedly had felt at the end of their lives. Maddux wasn't going to kill Theodore . . . but he was going to decimate his life as he currently knew it.

"Gentleman, have a seat," Maddux drawled cordially from his chair behind the massive mahogany desk dominating the room.

Two of his trusted men from his security team stood flanking the closed door behind Theodore and Gavin. In front of where Maddux was positioned were four comfortable leather chairs and one extra he'd situated next to his own so that Vincent could sit beside him and across from the two men who'd made most of their living by extorting money from too trusting citizens and small businesses that could barely make ends meet as it was. Maddux's parents being two of those people who'd suffered, and died, as a result of Theodore's and Gavin's greed.

Theodore huffed out an indignant breath that did little to disguise his rising apprehension as he glared from Maddux to Vincent. "What the hell kind of setup is this?"

Maddux leaned casually back in his chair and gave the other man a contemptuous smile. "Come on, Theodore," he mocked. "Did you really think you were invited to a very exclusive ball because you're the pillar of society? You clearly have a very large outstanding debt as a result of your gambling habit that's gotten out of control, and according to Vincent, your repayment, and accumulating interest, is past due. If you're unable to pay what you owe Vincent, then I'll be taking over the note and you'll be forced to meet *my* demands for compensation, and I can guarantee that by the time I'm done with you, you'll wish that you'd never crossed paths with me or my family."

"This is complete and utter bullshit," Gavin snarled like a rabid pit bull. "This is extortion and you won't get away with it."

Maddux laughed at the accusation. "That is fucking rich, coming from two men who've made a living extorting and killing innocent people who are barely able to make ends meet. Now sit. The. Fuck. *Down*." Each enunciated word reverberated in the room, angry and imposing enough that both Gavin and Theodore did as they were told, albeit begrudgingly.

An odd noise sounded on the other side of the door, and Maddux didn't hesitate to get up to make sure no one else was on the balcony level, which he'd made strictly off-limits tonight for this private meeting. One of his security guys stepped forward as a precaution, and as soon as Maddux opened the door, he was shocked to see Arabella standing on the other side.

The stricken look in her wide blue eyes told him that she'd heard what he'd said about her father being a criminal . . . and worse. Maddux clenched his jaw at this unexpected turn of events. He didn't want her here. She didn't belong here, where corruption was about to take place, where Maddux himself would be ruthless in his vengeance. Yet . . . didn't she deserve to know what a piece of shit her father really was?

And humiliating Theodore in front of his daughter was just another layer of revenge Maddux couldn't pass up.

"Bella," he murmured, deliberately softening the hatred and rage from his voice for her. "Since you've already been privy to our private conversation, why don't you come in and join us and hear the rest of it?"

Wringing her hands, she tentatively stepped

inside, her gaze immediately darting to Theodore. Pain and confusion etched across her pretty features and she swallowed hard before speaking. "Father . . . what have you done?" It came out as an aching whisper.

"I don't want her here," Theodore said through clenched teeth, ignoring the question and refusing to make eye contact with Arabella. "This has nothing to do with her."

"I'm your *daughter*," she said, more firmly now. "Whatever is going on with you, I have a right to know what it is."

"Stay out of this, Arabella," Gavin interjected, his tone condescending. "None of this concerns you."

She strode the few steps it took to stand in front of where the other man was sitting, her animosity toward Gavin nearly palpable. Her fingers flexed in front of her, as if she were holding back the temptation to slap him across the face for the superior way he talked to her. "If it concerns my father, then it concerns me. I'm not leaving."

With that, she settled into one of the vacant chairs, while Maddux returned to his seat behind his desk, resisting the urge to applaud her gumption.

"Let's get back to business," Maddux stated, leaning forward in his chair and clasping his hands on his desk.

He glanced at Vincent, indicating he had the

floor. He'd been good friends with the man sitting beside him for years. It had actually been Vincent's father, Christopher, who'd been a mentor to Maddux and had offered both financial advice and the capital to build his tech business. Unlike Theodore, Maddux had paid off his debt a long time ago. He didn't like owing anyone anything, and never would.

"As of tonight, I'm calling in your loan, Theodore," Vincent said without preamble.

"You can't do that." Theodore's voice was just short of begging.

"According to the contract you signed, I can," Vincent replied smugly, and slid a piece of paper across Maddux's desk that showed the other man's signature at the bottom. "I just did."

"I need more time." Sweat beaded at Theodore's receding hairline and trickled down the sides of his face, even though it was a cool sixty-eight degrees in the room. "It's not like I have one and a half million dollars sitting around at home!"

Arabella gasped at that revelation, her mouth gaping open at the staggering amount. She stared at Theodore in shock as the first of many truths started to unfold about her father.

"Let's be honest here," Vincent said calmly, even though Maddux knew, beneath that cool composure, his friend was a shark. "Because of your gambling habit, you barely have two dollars to rub together and every line of credit you own is maxed out. That's a problem for a businessman like me, especially with the interest you're accruing at a rapid pace based on the principal you owe me."

Theodore started to breathe a little bit harder as he dabbed a handkerchief across his sweaty forehead. "I've already signed over everything of value to you as collateral and a show of good faith," he said angrily.

Arabella made a soft, strangled sound in the back of her throat when she realized what was at stake . . . her and her father's entire livelihood, not to mention every piece of property they owned. "Father . . . no."

"I want the cash," Vincent demanded bluntly. "Tonight. Now."

"That's impossible and you know it," Gavin jumped to Theodore's defense.

"No, not impossible," Maddux drawled, causing three pairs of eyes to shift his way. Gavin's gaze narrowed, Theodore's gaze turned wary, and Arabella's eyes were filled with a hope he was going to crush. "Vincent, I'll purchase the debt, plus interest, in cash."

The look in Theodore's eyes turned wild, as if realizing the repercussions of that transfer. "*No*," he yelled, his voice shrill.

Ignoring the man's outburst, along with the distress written all over Arabella's face, Maddux retrieved the briefcase on the floor beside his chair and stood. After setting the attaché on the desk, he used a combination that released the locks, then opened the lid and turned the contents toward Vincent, just as they'd planned all along.

"How about three million dollars in cash in exchange for Theodore's promissory note, along with all his assets, signed over to me?"

"Jesus Christ," he heard Gavin say.

Theodore leapt up from his seat, his face white as a sheet at the implication of being at Maddux's mercy. "You *can't* do this!" he insisted frantically, panting for breath. "I don't have three million dollars and you can't just sell me off like some kind of cow to the highest bidder!"

"Did you not read the fine print in your contract?" Vincent asked, his tone blasé. "It clearly states that I have the right to sell your loan to another lender at any time without your consent." He stood up, snapped the briefcase shut, then held out a hand to Maddux for him to shake. "You have yourself a deal, Mr. Wilder. I'll be sure to have the transfer drawn up and the documents sent over to you on Monday for your approval and signature to formalize the deal. Theodore Cole's outstanding debt is now your headache to deal with, not mine."

Maddux watched Vincent leave the room, the first step toward sweet retribution flowing through him. For his mother and father, who'd moved to America from an impoverished town in Ireland because they'd wanted a better life for their family. Theodore was finally going to suffer until there was nothing left of him but a shell of a man. It was no less than the bastard deserved.

Theodore's hand went to the front of his dress shirt and pressed against his heaving chest. "You'll never get away with this, Wilder!"

Maddux gave him a cruel smile. "I already have. I *own* you, Theodore Cole. And I'm going to systematically ruin you and your life." He stood up and splayed his hands on the surface of his desk, knowing how imposing his height and stature made him look in that moment. "This is how it will go . . . First, I'm going to foreclose on your house and other properties you own. I will take all your fancy cars, including the classic ones you so dearly love. Your business partners will learn exactly what kind of men you and Gavin really are, and what you do on the side to supplement your income."

Theodore's eyes were huge with soul-deep despair, and he was sweating profusely now, his fingers tugging at the bow tie around his neck that had to be choking him. Maddux didn't give a shit, but it was the soft whimper of confusion and dismay that he heard from Arabella that nearly derailed everything he'd been planning for the past fourteen years. How could a woman he'd just met get under his skin in such a short amount of time?

Forcibly ignoring Arabella's distraught emotions, he finished putting the final nails in Theodore's coffin. "By the time I'm done wreaking havoc on your life, nobody will want anything to do with you. I'm going to take *everything* of value and importance away, so you'll no longer have the ability to take away from those less fortunate. You will *be* the less fortunate."

Theodore clutched at his heart, and a strangled sound escaped from his throat. Gavin turned toward the older man with concern, and before Theodore could fall back, Gavin grabbed his arm and eased him down onto the chair. Arabella immediately raced to her dad's side, frantically searching the front pockets of his tuxedo jacket for something.

"Father, where are your nitroglycerin pills?" she asked, clearly overwrought but also impressively in control of the situation, as if this wasn't the first time her father had had this kind of attack in her presence.

"Inside... pocket... jacket." He wheezed each word, and Arabella quickly found the medication, retrieved a small pill, and shoved it under her father's tongue.

"Jesus Christ, Wilder," Gavin yelled furiously. "He has a heart condition. You're giving him a fucking heart attack!"

Not an ounce of compassion stirred inside of Maddux. Feeling nothing but pure bitterness and disgust for the man, he merely crossed his arms over his chest and said nothing.

"I'll be fine," Theodore rasped, the medication that Arabella had given him seemingly calming his symptoms.

Arabella shook her head and turned toward Maddux with tears glimmering in her beautiful blue eyes. "Maddux . . . please . . ." she implored, so softly and so kindly even though he'd just announced his intentions to desecrate her dad. "Whatever my father has done to earn your wrath, you can't do this to him. He'll never survive. He's sick . . ." She took a step closer to his desk, brave and resolute despite the flicker of trepidation he saw in her gaze. "Take me instead."

Shock jarred through Maddux, but as a man who'd spent years perfecting a mask of control, neither his expression or body language betrayed that emotion. This woman was willing to give up her own freedom for her father's, and it was definitely an interesting turn of events he'd never seen coming.

"Arabella, *no*," her father uttered in horror.

Ignoring her father's objections, Arabella held Maddux's gaze steadily. "In exchange for you leaving my father alone, I will do whatever it takes, and whatever you demand, to work off his debt."

Her father moaned like a dying animal at his daughter's ultimate sacrifice, but other than that initial protest, he surprisingly said nothing more.

Maddux stared at the beautiful woman offering herself up to him, so sweet and naive in contrast to the dark, ruthless man he'd become. While he'd originally wanted to crush Theodore,

Maddux also realized that taking Arabella in exchange—his only daughter, who he adored—would be equally devastating to the other man. How could Theodore live with himself knowing Arabella belonged to his greatest enemy solely because of his own weakness?

"And how do you propose you work off your father's debt, Bella?" he asked, curious to hear her answer, especially when his own mind was already listing all the different ways he'd enjoy having her at his beck and call.

Bare shoulders held back, she swallowed hard, but her gaze remained bold and determined on his. "I will do *anything* you ask of me. I'm . . . I'm not afraid."

God, the woman was fucking fearless, he thought, and he was drawn to that courage despite himself. Unlike her father, or even Gavin, she was unwavering in her loyalty.

"For Christ's sake, Arabella," Gavin shouted angrily, his face contorted with rage. "He's not going to ask you to cook and clean and wash his laundry for him! He will *ruin* you for any other man."

Arabella turned her gaze to Gavin, her expression cool with resolve. "Then so be it. It's *my* choice to make."

Gavin clenched his jaw and shifted his hot, angry gaze to Maddux. "She clearly doesn't know what she's saying."

"I know *exactly* what I'm saying and what I'm

doing," she snapped at Gavin as she came to stand in front of him, poking her finger at his chest. "Unlike you, I'm willing to stand up and put my father's life and welfare before my own. I'll do whatever it takes to relieve him of this burden."

"*Arabella*," her father groaned, the sound filled with guilt. But for a second time, Theodore didn't try and talk Arabella out of the proposition she'd asked of Maddux.

The man was either truly very sick or fucking selfish as hell, Maddux thought.

When Gavin said nothing else, Arabella whirled around to face Maddux again, the skirt of her voluminous ball gown swirling around her legs. "I promise, you'll have no trouble from me. I will work off his debt, in any way you demand, in exchange for his freedom. Just . . . let him go. Please."

Maddux could have denied her request and forged full steam ahead with the original plan, but everything about Arabella intrigued and tempted him. He wanted her, desired her . . . plus there was the bonus of Theodore thinking the worst was happening while his only daughter was under his care. The things the man would conjure in his mind would rip any decent father apart inside.

Determined to keep the upper hand, Maddux strolled around his desk until he was standing in front of Arabella and she tipped her head back to meet his gaze, hers with bold resolve. She'd clearly meant what she said when she'd told him she wasn't afraid, and her tenacity made his dick twitch with the thought of taming that fiery attitude in the bedroom.

And make no mistake, that's exactly where he intended to have her, eventually.

Not giving a shit that both Theodore and Gavin watched, he reached out and brushed the backs of his fingers across Arabella's smooth, silken cheek, immensely pleased to see a heated awareness flicker in her gaze, proof that persuading her into his bed wasn't going to be all that difficult. She might hate him for what he held over her father, but she wasn't immune to the attraction between them.

"I'll accept your offer, Bella," he murmured, taking her chin between his thumb and forefinger, wanting this beautiful creature to look into his eyes and know exactly what he expected of her. Wanting to make sure there was no mistaking what she was about to trade. "Your father's freedom for your total surrender. That is the deal."

Her lips parted on a soft gasp at his bold, brazen request, and behind her, Gavin went ballistic at Maddux's offer. The other man tried to lunge at Maddux, but Mark, one of his security guys still standing at the door, was quicker and had Gavin's arms secured behind his back in no time flat, holding him back while Maddux continued.

"This is how it will go, Bella. I'm going to be gracious enough to allow your father to walk out of here tonight just as he arrived at the ball, still in debt and his assets signed over to me *until* I've decided you've fulfilled your part of the contract, but I will not ruin him tonight . . . as much as he deserves it." Not yet, anyway.

"No, but you *will* ruin her," Gavin shouted belligerently.

What was this, the eighteenth century? Gavin sounded like an ass and Maddux arched an insolent brow at the other man. "I'm not forcing her into this arrangement."

"Gavin, *stop*," Arabella insisted. "I am doing this of my own free will to save my father."

"Do you realize what he's demanding of you?" he asked, nearly frothing at the mouth with loathing, along with an unmistakable amount of heated jealousy.

She swallowed hard and nodded. "Yes."

Maddux allowed a sneer to curve the corner of his mouth as he met the daggers in Gavin's gaze. "Don't you think what I'm asking is a small price to pay for her father's and *your* sins?" He didn't enjoy exploiting Arabella, but for the sake of provoking Gavin, he made an exception. "Or maybe you'd like to tell Arabella exactly why you and Theodore are in this predicament to begin with?"

Gavin struggled against the guard's hold, all to no avail. "Bastard," he spat at Maddux.

"How long do you intend to keep my daughter?" Theodore asked, still sitting, his color looking slightly better than he had a few minutes ago, and his anger had returned.

Maddux wasn't sure if Theodore was more concerned about his daughter or the possibility of having his loan forgiven and his assets given back, which Maddux never intended to let happen. Not in this lifetime. "Three million dollars is a shit ton of money, Theodore," he drawled insolently, knowing his next words would undoubtedly inflame the other man. "It could take *years* to work off that kind of debt."

Theodore stood up, though he wasn't altogether steady on his feet. "You're a goddamn beast."

"And you, Arabella, are going to be his *whore*," Gavin said, lashing out to hurt her.

Maddux saw the shocked, hurt look on Arabella's face and he didn't hesitate to close the distance between himself and Gavin and wrap one big hand around the other man's throat. With his security guard still restraining Gavin, he squeezed tight until he nearly cut off Gavin's air supply and the man's eyes began to bulge. "If you *ever* talk to her like that again, I will bury you alive beneath five feet of concrete right down the street where the sidewalks are being torn up and renovated. Do you understand?" he asked succinctly.

Gavin tried to move his head, and Maddux

took that as a nod of agreement and released the other man, who immediately gasped for breath.

"Get them both out of here," Maddux ordered his security guys with a wave of his hand. "I want them off the premises immediately."

Mark dragged Gavin out of the office while he yelled out to Maddux, "You'll pay for this!", but before the other security guard could escort Theodore out, Arabella rushed to her father and pulled him into a hug.

"Don't worry about me," she assured him, her voice strong and steady. "I'll be fine. You need to take care of yourself. I love you and I'll be in touch so you'll know I'm okay."

The first inklings of remorse crept across Theodore's face, as if it was finally registering what his daughter was giving up for him. "You don't have to do this," he said gruffly.

A sad smile touched her lips. "There's no other alternative and we both know it," she said softly. "I just wish you would have told me about the debt before it got this bad."

Maddux watched Theodore go, thinking about all the deceit and lies the man had kept from his daughter all these years. If she knew all of the truth, she'd undoubtedly see her father in a whole different and unflattering light. He wondered if she would have so graciously offered herself in her dad's place if she'd known the blood Theodore had on his hands.

As soon as the other men were gone and the

door closed behind them so that he and Arabella were alone, she turned around to face him, beautifully, stunningly fearless, and a little defiant as she met his gaze.

And all Maddux could think was that his brother and sister were going to fucking kill him when they discovered what he'd done. That he'd allowed Theodore to walk away unscathed in exchange for a tiny slip of a woman Maddux wanted for himself.

His display of weakness rankled the hell out of him, and he embraced the spite he needed to keep his emotional distance from Arabella Cole when she was nothing more than a piece of collateral in this war between him and Theodore. Physically, however, all bets were off.

CHAPTER SIX

Now that Arabella was alone with Maddux, her initial bravado slipped a few notches and a good dose of wariness trickled through her as her captor held her gaze. His arms were crossed over his broad chest, which was more prominent now that he was no longer wearing his tuxedo jacket from earlier, and he'd taken off his bow tie for his meeting with her father. The first few buttons on his dress shirt were undone, giving her a more detailed glimpse of the scarred flesh on his neck, and he'd rolled his sleeves up, revealing strong, muscled forearms.

She exhaled a deep breath as the charged silence stretched between them, his expression hardening with animosity. Arabella didn't question offering herself to this dark, commanding man in exchange for allowing her father to safely walk out of this room, because her dad's health and well-being were what mattered the most to her right now. After everything she'd just heard and witnessed, and the accusations that had been verbalized, she had no doubt her father was far from a saint. But with his age and his heart condition, she knew he'd never survive the stress of everything Maddux had just threatened him with, and she'd offered up the only thing she could think of that might interest a man like Maddux. Herself. In any capacity he desired.

However, Arabella was smart enough to realize that all the resentment and bitterness Maddux harbored toward her dad had not magically disappeared just because he'd accepted her proposal. He still held every single one of her father's assets hostage, and there was no guarantee that he'd ever relinquish them. But this arrangement at least gave her time to try and figure out a way to get her father out of the mess he'd created for himself. If there was a possibility, she had to try.

Which meant she now belonged to Maddux Wilder. Her life. Her body. Her entire world. She was his to do with as he pleased, and while Arabella was certain she was just a temporary diversion for a powerful man like him, a plaything, and possibly a pawn to use to hurt her father, there was no denying the heat and lust in his eyes when he looked at her. And as much as she wanted to despise him, her traitorous body was inexplicably drawn to Maddux and shamelessly wanted him in ways she'd never desired another man.

"Having second thoughts, Bella?" he asked, his tone mocking, as if he was trying to provoke her or see how far he could push her before she'd break.

"No." She tipped her chin up, showing her obstinate side. She might be small and petite, but she was not fragile, emotionally or physically. "I don't renege on my promises."

He inclined his dark head arrogantly, causing a few long, unruly strands of his hair to fall across his forehead as his mouth twisted sardonically. "Good to know, considering what it's going to take for you to work off your father's debt."

There was a thread of anger in his voice, whether at her or at himself, she wasn't quite sure, but she stood her ground and didn't wither beneath his increasingly irritable glare.

His jaw clenched and he strode to the door and opened it before glancing back at her. "Let's escort you to your new living quarters, shall we."

It wasn't so much a question as it was a demand. For her, the fairy-tale ball was over, and Arabella had a feeling she wasn't going to be living happily ever after any time soon. She walked out of the office, and Maddux took her elbow and directed her toward an elevator on that same floor. He inserted what looked to be a security key card, and the double doors slid open, allowing them inside the surprisingly plush lift.

She had no idea where Maddux was taking her and didn't bother asking since it didn't really matter and she had no say in the situation anyway. Her "living quarters" could be a dump or a dungeon with bars for all she knew. He pressed a button with a capital *M* etched on it, which was above a button with an *H* and another with a *T*.

As the elevator gradually made its way upward and past each floor in the district warehouse, her stomach definitely twisted and turned with a bout of silent nerves, because no matter how she looked at things, her life was about to undergo some major alterations, and she had no say over any of the changes about to happen or the demands that Maddux made. She'd given herself to him of her own free will.

The elevator finally came to a smooth stop at what appeared to be the top floor of the building, and when the double doors slid open, Arabella was shocked to see that they'd arrived at what looked to be a luxurious, palatial apartment, with black marble floors and an entryway that transitioned to a spacious open-concept living room, dining room, and state-of-the-art kitchen. Everything was black and chrome and leather, the décor sleek, minimal, and masculine.

"What is this place?" she asked quietly.

"My penthouse, where I live. Follow me," he said, his tone brusque. "I'm not in the mood to give you a tour of the place. You can familiarize yourself with everything tomorrow while I'm out for the day."

Alrighty then. She followed him down a hallway off the living room, passing a few closed doors, until they reached a bedroom big enough to host a small party in. The black and chrome and leather theme continued, and there was no overlooking the huge, king-sized poster bed dominating a good portion of the room. The mattress was so high off the ground compared to her petite height, she'd almost need a small set of steps to help boost herself up, or a running start to jump on top.

"This is where you will stay and sleep," he informed her, his expression and attitude still terse. "There is a master ensuite for your use, as well."

She turned to face him. "Is this . . . umm . . . a guest room?"

That beautiful mouth of his slanted with callous amusement. "No, sweet, naïve Bella. It's *my* room. Trust me, the bed is plenty big enough for two. I didn't exchange you for three million dollars for you to have a fun sleepover in the guest bedroom."

She exhaled a deep breath. *Okay, fair enough*, she thought, realizing that there was no reprieve for her. No easing into the situation or a courtship leading up to the sex part of their agreement. Romance of any kind was not a part of this package deal.

"Make yourself comfortable," he said, his voice as cool and indifferent as his demeanor. "I'll be in my office on the other side of the apartment, and I don't want to be bothered. We'll go over rules and more general expectations of your duties in the morning."

He quickly spun around to leave, as if he couldn't get away fast enough, but she wasn't ready to let him go just yet. "Wait," she blurted out before he cleared the bedroom door. "I have one question for you."

Body tense, he abruptly stopped and slowly faced her again. He said nothing, his expression frustratingly blank, but she took advantage of the fact that he'd actually acknowledged her request, even if only silently.

"What, exactly, did my father do to deserve this treatment and your hatred?" she asked.

He was quiet for long moments, as if debating whether or not to spill the truth. "You'll have to ask *him* that question," he said, clearly wanting her dad to give her the cold, hard facts. "Just know this... Theodore Cole is not the man he's portrayed himself to be to you. You have *no* idea who your father really is or what he's capable of."

She was beginning to believe that was true, but instead of acknowledging Maddux's statement, she boldly tossed it right back in his face. "That's what Gavin said about you. That you're a dangerous, malicious man."

"Did he now?" He arched a dark brow as he leisurely started walking back toward her, though his disposition was anything but casual. "He's right, Bella. I'm vindictive, merciless. And fucking ruthless."

The words were a low, mean snarl and she swallowed hard and held her ground as he neared, crowding into her personal space. Her breathing kicked up a notch, causing the upper swells of her breasts, pushed up by the corset stays in her dress, to quiver ever so slightly—her only outward sign of unease. She resisted the urge to step back, and considering he was essentially towering over her, she had to tip her head back to look up at his face, which was stunningly gorgeous, despite the animosity etching his features.

"Considering everything *I* am, are you afraid of me?" he asked, his tone harsh and provoking.

She'd already told him she wasn't scared in his office, and that still held true despite his boorish behavior now. "No."

A spiteful smile curled the corners of his mouth. "Maybe you should be."

The light amber hue of his eyes had grown dark and turbulent, and still that didn't change the fact that, while she might be a tad bit nervous about the unknown quantities of her confinement and everything it entailed, she wasn't frightened, nor did she feel unsafe with him. Maybe that *was* too naïve and trusting of her, but this big, assertive, dominating man standing in front of her had already proven to be a contradiction and she wanted to trust the *good* she'd seen in him.

Twice he'd already defended her honor... the first time when they'd been dancing down at the ball and Gavin had roughly grabbed her arm, and again when Gavin had called her a whore and Maddux had nearly ripped his throat out for his disparaging comment. Arabella had to believe a man who didn't hesitate to protect a woman, especially one connected to his greatest enemy, wasn't looking to deliberately hurt her physically. After everything that had transpired downstairs in his office, he had his own walls up, and his anger was out in full force. He was lashing out, and she was currently taking the brunt of his resentment. He hated her for her father's sins, but on a gut-deep level, she knew Maddux wasn't a man to abuse any woman—despite his threat that she should fear him.

"What are you going to do to me?" she asked in a soft voice, more curious than worried.

His gaze fell to her lips, then traveled down to her chest, a flicker of hunger igniting in his eyes when they met hers again. "Anything. *Everything*. I told you I expect your total surrender, and I meant it."

"Will you take me by force?" Yes, she'd just assured herself that he wasn't a cruel man, but she wanted and needed to hear the truth from his own mouth.

His jaw clenched at her question, and his brows slashed angrily, as if she'd thoroughly insulted him. "I've *never* forced a woman to do anything she didn't want to, and I'm not about to start with you. Anything that happens between us will be consensual and because it's what you want and desire. But make no mistake, Bella, I will have you in my bed, and not just to sleep. I will have your sweet mouth wrapped around my cock and your body milking mine when I'm buried deep inside your pussy."

Her lips parted and her entire face flushed red hot with shock. The dirty, filthy words should have offended her—it was what he probably intended—but instead they aroused her. Her tightening nipples scratched against the fabric of her gown, and the slick moisture she felt between her legs was in direct response to his explicit and vivid statement.

His gaze narrowed slightly. "Have you ever been kissed?" he asked abruptly, obviously mistaking her blush and speechless response for total innocence.

"Of course I have," she replied indignantly.

He smirked at her snappy retort. "Have you ever been fucked?"

She should have expected that blunt, crude question, but he once again managed to steal her ability to form a quick comeback. That, and her face was once again turning bright pink with the fact that she had to admit, at age twenty-five, she still owned her V-card.

"Answer me," he demanded impatiently.

"No," she said with a shake of her head as her fingers anxiously twisted in the fabric that made up the skirt of her gown. "I've never been with a man that way."

His nostrils flared ever so slightly with that realization, and there was no mistaking the possessive spark of heat that flared in his gaze, making her entire body hyperaware of the fact that he owned her and her virginity.

"Are you saving yourself for marriage?" he asked.

"No." Remaining celibate for this long had never been a conscious choice, it was just the way things had worked out. "I just never got that far with any of the guys I've dated." In fact, most of her relationships had been incredibly short-lived and she'd always wondered why, since those men always abruptly ended things without a reason or explanation.

"Not even Gavin." It wasn't a question, but rather a gloating statement of fact.

Despite the situation, she couldn't stop the small smile that tugged at the corner of her mouth. "Oh, he's tried a few of the times we've gone out, but I'd rather eat a whole jar of jalapeño peppers than allow him to touch me like that." She shuddered at the thought, then met his gaze more seriously. "I'd like to think my virginity should be worth something to help reduce my father's debt."

He shrugged, back to masking his true feelings in an indifferent façade. "A couple thousand, I suppose."

She winced at his deliberately insensitive remark. Okay, *that* hurt, but what did she expect from a man who held such a deeply ingrained grudge against her father? Clearly, her virginity held no great value to him and she was nothing more than a warm female body to sate his baser desires.

"Well, I suppose a couple thousand dollars is a start toward that repayment," she said, trying to make light of the situation.

He didn't look amused. In fact, he suddenly looked very fierce and intense. "No, *this* is a start," he growled low and deep in his throat.

Quick and sudden, his hand shot out and she gasped as he shoved his fingers into the loose knot of hair swept back and secured against the nape of her neck. A few pins holding the intricate style in place jostled loose, hitting the marbled floor with soft metallic pings as he used his grip on those strands to pull her head back. His lips came crashing down on hers in a searing invasion that was far from sweet, gentle, or romantic.

Arabella's hands came up to his chest, not to push him away but to curl her fingers into the material of his shirt so she had something to hold on to for this wild, seductive ride unlike anything she'd ever experienced before. She did nothing to stop him or the aggressive, all-consuming kiss that immediately ignited dark and forbidden desires inside her. The kind of brazen and wicked yearnings that should have shamed her because Maddux was ultimately *her* enemy, as well.

But there was no denying the growing ache between her legs as his mouth ravished hers, or the knowledge that giving herself over to this man was going to be far easier, and possibly more enjoyable, than she'd ever imagined.

CHAPTER SEVEN

MADDUX MEANT TO punish Arabella with his hard, contentious kiss, or at the very least instill a healthy dose of fear in her, even though he knew both impulses were pretty fucked up. Then again, *he* was feeling pretty fucked up after all that had gone down in his office and the lengths to which he'd been forced to go for the repayment he demanded of her father.

But ultimately it didn't really matter what he intended, because his plan quickly backfired mere seconds after his mouth had claimed hers and she'd willingly yielded to his demanding assault on her senses, allowing him to release all the frustration, pain, and anger brewing inside of him for the past hour. He unleashed all those turbulent emotions on her in the deep, hungry, greedy thrust of his tongue and the deliberate, relentless way he plundered her mouth. The same way he wanted to plow hard and deep into her body.

A part of him wanted her to fight him, to hit him, to shove him away and slap his face for being so barbaric with her—anything to make resisting her more difficult. But this sweet submission of hers . . . it was nearly his undoing after the shitty way he'd treated her. He deserved her fury, not her capitulation.

Instead, she swayed into him of her own accord, her breasts pressing against his chest and her lush, soft lips pliant beneath his as he swept his tongue deep inside her mouth. She trembled and moaned, not in pain but with a need and hunger that matched the one burning him up inside. His cock thickened and throbbed relentlessly, and it took every ounce of control he possessed not to back her up against the nearest wall, hike up her dress, rip off her panties, and fuck her so hard he'd forget everything that had transpired tonight but the sheer, mindless ecstasy of taking what was now his.

Somehow, through the haze of lust fogging his mind, he managed to remind himself that she wasn't one of his normal conquests who knew and enjoyed just how dominant he liked to get in the bedroom. She was a *virgin*, for Christ's sake. Yet the thought of being the first man to show her how good a cock could feel thrusting in and out of her desire-slickened pussy, and being the one to make her scream in pure pleasure as she came all over his shaft, was like an irresistible temptation that was beginning to override common sense.

Forcing himself to stop, he tore his mouth from hers, and her lashes slowly fluttered open, revealing blue eyes that were so fucking trusting he felt as though someone had punched him in the gut. Despite being warned and shown how merciless and cold-hearted he could be, and despite that unrelenting kiss that was only a preview to his more uncivilized side, she was looking up at him with damp, kiss-swollen lips and like she wanted *more* of what he'd just doled out.

Grabbing her arms, he gently but firmly pushed her away, and it was that deliberate separation, combined with the purposeful scowl he gave her, that effectively snapped her out of the dreamy trance she seemed to have fallen into and jerked her back to the reality of the situation.

Good. Because he wasn't any kind of Prince Charming here to save the day, despite the fairytale ball she'd attended. No, he was the villain and the beast in this scenario and that would never change.

"Go to bed," he ordered in a harsh tone, and spun around on his heel and left the room, slamming the door shut behind him so hard the walls vibrated—and hopefully helped to instill some much-needed apprehension in Arabella.

He headed straight to his office at the opposite end of his penthouse, immediately poured himself a hefty amount of the bourbon he'd shared with his brother and sister earlier in a toast to Theodore's demise—which Maddux had royally screwed up—and downed every last drop in one long swallow. He welcomed the burn of alcohol as it seared its way down his throat and spread throughout his belly like fire as he added at least another four shots to the glass in his attempt to get shit-faced.

How could a plan that should have been so simple and easy to execute have gone so fucking wrong? Instead of destroying Theodore Cole, he'd given the man a reprieve... and as Maddux tossed back another drink, he swore that's all it would be, and a brief one at that because he'd made no promises to relinquish Theodore's debt or assets. Taking Arabella was definitely a form of vengeance... just not one his brother and sister had anticipated.

"Fuck," he muttered beneath his breath, hating himself for being so weak and for letting Arabella derail his plans. Maddux's siblings had counted on him, had trusted him to extract the revenge fourteen years in the making, and he'd let them down.

Not ready to face his brother's and sister's disappointment and outrage for the choice he'd made, Maddux pulled his cell phone from his pocket. He sent Hunter and Tempest a brief joint text before they tried contacting him first, or worse, came to his penthouse tonight when Maddux wasn't in the frame of mind to explain his decision.

It's done. I'll talk to you both in the morning.

Yeah, it was done, all right, he thought sarcastically as he tossed his phone onto his desk and walked to the floor-to-ceiling windows in his office that overlooked the city. He finished the rest of the bourbon, grateful to finally feel a buzz settling in, taking the edge off the strong urge to put a fist through the wall in anger and frustration for the idiotic choice he'd made tonight.

Instead, his conversation with Arabella in his bedroom filtered through his increasingly fuzzy mind. She'd point-blank asked him what her father had done to earn Maddux's rage, and instead of taking the opportunity to shatter her perfect illusion of her father's character by revealing the truth, he'd evaded the question, because he wanted Theodore to have to confess to his daughter the kind of life he led, the people he'd bullied, and the few he'd even killed.

Maddux laughed bitterly because he knew in reality Theodore would never admit to any transgressions that would tarnish his reputation, which meant at some point, Maddux *would* enlighten Arabella. It was the kind of bombshell to drop when he was done with her and decided to give her back to her father ... who'd so easily given up his daughter in hopes of having his debt forgiven. Maddux could only hope that finding out what kind of monster her father really was would essentially destroy the relationship between Arabella and Theodore.

In the meantime, Maddux had a twenty-five-year-old virgin in his bed—and a feisty, gutsy one at that. Learning she'd never slept with a man before shouldn't have surprised him, considering he was aware—based on the weekly PI reports he received—that Gavin had managed to scare off any guy who'd shown Arabella the slightest bit of romantic interest.

A sardonic smirk twisted across Maddux's lips as he gazed out the window and slowed his alcohol consumption down to smaller sips now that the effects of the bourbon had calmed him considerably. Gavin clearly wanted Arabella's innocence for himself, and how ironic was it that her virtue now belonged to Maddux, which had to be driving the other man absolutely insane. And judging by her eager response to his hot, aggressive kiss, and witnessing the desire in her eyes after the fact, there was no denying that seducing Arabella would be far easier than Maddux had anticipated.

A few hours later, with Maddux drunk enough to have drowned out all the recriminations he'd heaped upon himself for the night's events, he stumbled his way back to his bedroom. He stopped at the closed door for a few seconds, preparing himself to deal with Arabella, but when he finally stepped inside, he was surprised to find that she wasn't awake as he'd braced himself for, even though he *had* ordered her to go to bed.

Instead, he found her asleep on top of his king-sized mattress. Having removed his shoes in his office, he moved quietly into the room, and since she'd left one of the nightstand lamps on, he was able to see her, even if his vision was a little blurred around the edges from all the liquor he'd consumed. He stopped at the opposite side of the bed from where she was dozing, narrowing his gaze for better focus. As he registered the way her tiny body was curled into a fetal position, along with the dark, exhausted smudges beneath her eyes and the way the strands of her hair that he'd dislodged with his hands earlier fell across her beautiful face, something unfamiliar and oddly protective stirred in his chest.

Fucking alcohol was messing with his head and his emotions.

She was still wearing her elaborate ball gown because she obviously had nothing else to sleep in, which couldn't have been comfortable, along with her heels that peeked from beneath the hem of her dress. Her hands were tucked under her cheek on the pillow, her soft lips parted as she inhaled and exhaled deep, even breaths. All curled up, she looked so small and vulnerable and defenseless, even though he'd seen for himself what a tough, strong-willed, and stubborn little spitfire she'd been during her father's ordeal, and even after that when she'd dealt with Maddux alone.

But silently watching her now, with his animosity and bitterness dulled by alcohol, he was hit hard by the knowledge that she'd been through an enormous and unexpected emotional trauma tonight, and he'd been nothing short of a hostile asshole who'd lashed out at her for her father's sins. She'd undoubtedly come to the fairy-tale ball expecting to enjoy a fun, fanciful evening and had ended up a prisoner to a man who wanted to hate her... but he just couldn't summon the contempt.

He rubbed his forehead wearily, then before he could change his bourbon-soaked mind, he retrieved one of his T-shirts from the closet, then walked around the big four-poster bed to where Arabella was dozing. Her back was now facing him, and wanting to at least make her comfortable while she slept, he first removed her heels, then started unzipping her dress from where it began mid-back, all the way down to the base of her spine, until the fabric loosened from her body.

The first thing that registered was all that soft, creamy-looking skin he wanted to caress with his fingers, or even better yet, lower his head and skim his lips from her bare shoulders down to the curve of her ass, where a pair of cream-colored lace panties settled on her hips. Steeling himself against the rush of heat that went straight to his aching groin, he gently rolled her to her back and began working the sleeves and the bodice of her dress down her arms and chest.

She moaned softly, her lashes slowly fluttering open. Confused, disoriented eyes stared up at him, and he immediately stopped removing her gown, because the last thing he wanted Arabella to think was that he was trying to take advantage of her. He might have been a grade-A bastard to her earlier tonight, but he'd meant what he said when he'd told her he'd never force her.

Her head tipped drowsily to the side on the pillow, a frown creasing her brow. "What are you doing?"

There was no panic in her voice, just a calm, trusting curiosity that slayed him. "Putting you in something more comfortable to sleep in," he said, his tone gruff. "Is that okay?"

She blinked up at him, still seemingly half-asleep. "I don't have my nightgown."

"I know." He felt the slightest tug of a smile at how cute she was, then managed to suppress it before it fully formed. "You can wear one of my T-shirts for now." Tomorrow, he'd send for her clothes and other personal items.

"Thank you." She sighed with gratitude. "The top of the dress was tight."

She sat up and pushed the voluptuous gown down her petite form, kicking off all those layers of fabric with her feet. Maddux sucked in a quick breath. Jesus Christ, she wasn't wearing a bra. Nor was she particularly modest about exposing her small, pert breasts and barely there underwear . . . or maybe she was so emotionally and mentally tired that she didn't realize how complacent she currently was, or she just didn't care.

But to him, she was pure, sinful temptation, and he quickly yanked his T-shirt over her head and arranged it to her thighs. Then he pulled down the covers so she could slip between the sheets and comforter, and she didn't hesitate to snuggle into his bed as though she fucking *belonged* there.

When he was certain she'd drifted off to slumber again, he removed his own clothes down to his boxer briefs, then settled onto his side of the mattress, though there was a good four feet between them. He reached over and switched off the nightstand light, then tried to relax enough to let the last remnants of alcohol lull him to a nice, passed-out state of sleep. It was probably the only peace he was going to get for a good while.

He was nearly there when Arabella's soft, husky voice jarred him awake.

"Maddux?"

He turned his head on the pillow to look at her, but her face was in shadows and he couldn't see her expression. "Yes?" he replied, his tone brusque, mostly because he was annoyed that she'd made his body completely aware of her all over again.

He heard her exhale a soft breath. "Whatever my father did to you and your family . . . I want you to know that I'm very sorry."

Well, shit. What the hell did he say to that sincere acknowledgement and apology? It wasn't her fault that, beneath her father's expensive suits and fancy trappings, Theodore was nothing more than a cruel, cold-blooded, self-centered man. But responding with a pat *it's okay* response wasn't going to happen, either, because no amount of contrition would ever change the past or bring Maddux's parents back or be enough to forgive her father for his heartless, vindictive ways.

So, he evaded the issue all together. "Go to sleep, Bella," he said, and was grateful when he was met with blessed silence.

CHAPTER EIGHT

Arabella had no idea what time it was when she finally woke up the following morning. There were no clocks in Maddux's room, and her cell phone, which she'd kept in a hidden pocket that had been sewn into her gown so she didn't have to carry a purse all night at the ball, was somewhere tangled up in the heap of material on the floor . . . while she was wearing one of Maddux's T-shirts.

She could have gotten out of bed to retrieve her phone, but moving in any way meant risking awakening her bedmate, who was sleeping on his side, facing her. And right now, with the light of day streaming in through the glass slider leading to a master suite terrace, Maddux looked so calm and peaceful without animosity and anger slashing across his face and blazing in his eyes.

He was a stunningly gorgeous man. His features were perfectly defined and masculine, but in slumber, all those rough edges were softer, the harsh clench of his jaw now relaxed. His lips looked full and sensual, and her stomach tumbled with awareness when she thought about that hot, provocative kiss they'd shared.

His dark, longish hair was a tousled mess around his head, and morning stubble covered his jawline, which only added to how attractive and sexy he was. The covers were bunched around his waist, and since he was without clothes, she had an unobstructed view of his broad shoulders, his wide, muscled chest, and the impressive bicep in his arm that looked as big as a melon, even unflexed.

He was utterly flawless... except for the large, unsightly scar on the side of his neck that ran down his shoulder and encompassed part of his arm. Whatever had happened to cause that now healed wound, it had to have been painful and hellish, because his skin was disfigured enough in that one area to indicate some kind of major trauma at some point in his life.

Her heart tightened in compassion at the horrible thought, at the possible agony he'd suffered. Without thinking of consequences, she reached out and lightly brushed her fingers along the marred flesh that covered the curve of his shoulder, as if touching it might lessen the severity of whatever had caused the multiple scars.

Belying his restful pose, Maddux's fingers instantly grabbed her wrist and jerked her hand away at the same time his eyes fully opened, looking directly at her, his gaze far more cognizant than she would have thought.

"*Don't.*"

The one-word warning was sharp enough to cut glass, and she swallowed hard but didn't flinch or cower. "Does it . . . hurt?"

His mouth twisted sardonically. "Not physically."

Which left emotional and mental pain still on the table. Clearly, there were unpleasant memories attached to those scars, and whatever they were, Maddux wasn't inclined to share. Then again, so far Maddux hadn't struck her as the kind of man who opened up easily about any part of his life.

He released her hand and immediately got out of bed. Without a word, he went into the bathroom, shut the door, and returned a few minutes later. Ignoring her, he went to a chest of drawers, retrieved a pair of jeans, and pulled them on over his black boxer briefs.

"When you're ready, I'll meet you in the kitchen for breakfast and to go over a few ground rules for living here."

And with that, he was gone. She exhaled a sigh, rolled to her back, and stared up at the ceiling, realizing that this was going to be her new normal for however long Maddux decided to keep her. A life with guidelines and rules and getting whiplash from his shifting moods. Oh, joy.

Last night, after he'd stormed out of the bedroom after kissing her, she'd had the thought that she could have walked out of his penthouse and left him and the situation behind. She could have called authorities and claimed kidnapping or tried any other number of ways to escape, but there was one thing that was most at stake that made her determined to remain and serve whatever sentence Maddux had in store for her.

She wasn't staying because of the possibility of having her father's massive debt forgiven, or the chance of Maddux releasing all her dad's assets back to him, because there was no guarantee of either. No, it was ultimately her father's declining health that kept her from walking away. Because if she didn't stay, she knew things would be worse for her dad, and the thought of losing her only parent—even if he *had* wronged Maddux and his siblings—was distressing enough to make Arabella follow through on the agreement she'd made.

She'd made a deal, and she would honor it.

With that pep talk, she got out of bed and went to the enormous bathroom that was half the size of the bedroom and like a luxurious spa. On one side was a long, sleek vanity with a heated towel rack at the end and some kind of fancy toilet. Opposite that wall was a huge glass-enclosed and marbled cubicle that combined numerous overhead showerheads and massage jets built into the wall, along with a gigantic soaking tub that had to have been custom-made to accommodate Maddux's size. Even if he spilled water over the rim, there were numerous drains on the floor to catch it all.

Considering how much Arabella loved baths, she'd at least enjoy that bit of luxury while she was here, she thought with a smile.

But right now, she had orders to meet Maddux in the kitchen, but as she stared into the bathroom mirror, she realized she had no clean clothes to change into, no makeup remover or even a brush for her hair. Until she retrieved some of her own things from home, she improvised by wiping away the smudges beneath her eyes with a tissue, brushed her teeth with her finger, and tried to tame her disheveled hair before joining Maddux in the luxurious kitchen, still wearing the T-shirt he'd put her in last night.

The delicious scent of bacon and coffee made her stomach grumble, and she found her captor standing at the stainless-steel stove, cooking the strips of pork. The sight of Maddux's bare, toned physique distracted her for a moment. His skin was tanned and smooth, and the way his muscled back tapered from his wide shoulders down to his narrow hips was nothing short of a work of art. The kind she could admire for hours for all its perfection.

He must have heard or sensed her presence, because he glanced over his shoulder to look at her. His expression was neutral, which she supposed was an improvement from last night's irate mood and this morning's grumpy disposition.

"There's orange juice, or fresh coffee if you

prefer," he said, returning his gaze to his task. "Creamer is in the refrigerator."

"Okay," she said, and went straight for the caffeine.

Since he had a cup already filled with coffee near him by the stove, she assumed the extra one on the counter was for her and poured the steaming brew into the mug. She added a spoonful of sugar from the glass dish he'd set out and a dollop of creamer to smooth out the taste.

She took a few sips, savoring the bold flavor before asking, "Can I help you with anything?"

"No. Sit at the counter." He pointed a finger toward the nearby kitchen nook area. "The bacon is almost crisp, and after that I'll scramble some eggs. Is that an acceptable breakfast for you?"

"Yes. Of course," she said, sliding onto one of the chrome and leather stools. "I'm not a fussy eater."

"Good to know." He removed the bacon from the frying pan, then heated up a clean one with a slice of butter for the eggs. "There's a pen and pad of paper right there in front of you. Make a list of what you like to eat, and anything else you want or need, and I'll get it ordered and delivered later today."

Ahh, the ease of online shopping. She picked up the pen and jotted down a few of her favorite snacks and things she could make for her lunches to take to work, which she needed to talk to him about at some point. She might be indebted to him for the foreseeable future, but she still had obligations and commitments to fulfill.

"Other than breakfast, do you have anyone who cooks for you or provides meals?" she asked curiously.

"No." He poured a bowl of beaten eggs into the buttered pan. "I have a housekeeper who comes in once a week on Thursdays, but when it comes to cooking, I'm pretty self-sufficient." He looked her way with a slight, rare smile. "And if I'm not in the mood to make something myself, there's always Grubhub."

Spoken like a true bachelor, she thought in amusement. "I'd like to make dinners if that's okay?" she asked, because it was something she enjoyed. "I'm pretty creative and I'm used to cooking for myself and Father on a regular basis, so I might as well make myself useful here."

Another deliberate glance her way revealed eyes that were dark and hot as they dropped to her mouth. "Bella, I'll make sure you're *plenty* useful," he murmured huskily.

She shivered, and it wasn't with trepidation, but anticipation. Her traitorous nipples tightened against the T-shirt she wore, and he smirked as his brazen gaze lowered and noticed her body's reaction. God, she was absolutely shameless when it came to this man, and at least the attraction was completely mutual.

He returned his attention to their breakfast and scooped some of the scrambled eggs onto two separate plates, one of the dishes heaped double the size of the other serving for himself, along with strips of bacon.

"I'll be sending two of my security guys to collect your things from your father's. They should be here by this afternoon," he said, changing the subject. "If there is anything that is missing once your personal effects arrive, let me know and I'll make sure it's retrieved."

He set a dish in front of where she was sitting, while he remained standing on the other side of the counter, facing her. She picked up her fork and pushed it through her fluffy eggs. "I can always go by myself and collect what I need."

"No." His voice was adamant, as was the implacable gleam in his eyes. "While you're under my authority, you may call and talk to your father on the phone, but any visits with him or to your home will be supervised."

Startled by the vehemence in his tone, she blinked at him. "Why?"

"Because I don't trust him to be alone with you," he replied succinctly. "And right now, until I decide differently, you're *mine*."

She opened her mouth to argue how ridiculous that demand was, but he gave his head a firm shake and cut her off. "*My* rules, Bella," he said, his voice a low, uncompromising growl. "And you *will* abide by them."

She bristled at his boorish attitude. If he expected her to turn into a meek and passive female at the snap of his fingers, he was about to learn, if he hadn't already, that her small stature didn't mean she was docile. "And if I don't?" she dared.

He slowly set his fork down on his plate as the corner of his mouth curled into a wicked smile that was both a threat and a promise. "Then it would be my pleasure to punish you accordingly. Don't underestimate the persuasion of a good, hard spanking, Bella. Trust me, the burn of my handprint on your smooth, bare ass will be a stark reminder *for days* of why it's not in your best interest to defy me."

Gulp. Her face flamed and she stared at him wide-eyed, stunned to realize that the thought of being bent over his lap and feeling the smack of his palm against her tender flesh actually made her squirm restlessly on the barstool. Holy crap, was she one of those women who'd *enjoy* being dominated by a man sexually? Or got off on experiencing a little pain with their pleasure? She couldn't deny the images in her head definitely aroused her.

"Any other issues with my orders?" he asked calmly as he took a bite of his crispy bacon, his too casual attitude belying the undercurrents of lust flowing between them. "Or maybe you'd like to sass me one more time and find out what I'd like to do to that warm, lush mouth of yours to remind you who is in charge here?" he challenged.

She absently bit her bottom lip, which, in hindsight, probably wasn't the smartest idea considering how avidly he was staring at her mouth just *hoping* she'd oppose him. God, what did it say about her that she was tempted to issue a smart-ass remark just because she was curious to know what it was like to submit to such a powerful man? The thought of giving herself over to Maddux's desires made her weak in the knees.

She smartly remained quiet, and he took her silence for compliance.

Maddux went back to eating his scrambled eggs, as if he hadn't just turned her inside out with a shameless kind of wanting. "So, now that you understand the repercussions of defying me or any of my orders, here is your own personal key card to the building and the elevator," he said, putting the credit-card-like piece of plastic next to her on the counter that already had her name on it. "When you use the key card, it will notify me when you come and go from the penthouse or the building and what floors you might stop on with the elevator. Tempest and Hunter live on the two levels below mine, and if they aren't home or don't want visitors, they can lock out their floor, as can I."

All Arabella could think about was the fact that this key card essentially had a tracker on it. And why not, since MadX-Tech was the king of all things security? "So, basically you'll be stalking me?" she asked wryly.

"No, not stalking," he replied, unoffended by her comment. "I'm going to keep track of you, because you're an asset and I always protect what's mine, Bella. You're no exception." Finished with his breakfast, he pushed his empty plate aside.

"And what about work?" she asked, feeling more exasperated by his restrictions, even though she'd willingly signed up for this. "I have a job and I don't want to give it up." She'd go stark raving mad if she had to sit around in this pristine penthouse castle all day and night.

"I wouldn't expect you to give up your position as a digital data analyst and curator at the university library," he said, stunning her with the fact that he knew her job description and where she was employed. "You'll be assigned a private security detail who will be with you at *all* times when you leave this building, and he'll make sure you're dropped off safely at work and picked up when you're done, as well. He'll report directly to me."

"That is ridiculous and unnecessary," she said, the irritable words slipping from her before she could censor them.

He arched a brow and crossed his arms over his chest, his stance more imposing now. "This isn't a negotiation, sweetheart. If you don't like my rules, you're free to leave."

Maddux's comment was casual, but it was the hard look in his eyes that told Arabella that if she walked out, her father's life would collapse as a result, and she wasn't ready or willing to take that chance. She'd knowingly traded her life for her father's, and this unsparing man in front of her wouldn't let her go without exacting some kind of vengeance from her father in return.

"Okay, fine." She pasted on a fake smile, but her annoyance remained and she couldn't keep it from seeping into her voice. "Your rules, your way, Mr. Wilder. Got it." She even saluted him for good measure. "Maybe you might even want to inject me with one of those human tracking devices just to be on the safe side."

Her deliberate impudence made his golden-brown eyes flare with something so searingly hot and purposeful it stole her breath and sent warning signals throughout her body.

"Last night I thought I was dealing with a sweet, compliant female. But today this impertinent mouth of yours is pushing all my fucking buttons," he murmured, shaking his head as he slowly rounded the counter toward her, each step ratcheting up her rapidly beating pulse, especially when she caught sight of the solid, immense column of flesh outlining the front of his jeans.

Clearly, the buttons she was pushing were purely sexual ones.

When he stood next to Arabella, he grabbed her chin between his fingers and tipped her head back so she was forced to look into his blazing eyes. "I seriously think your mouth is begging to be taught what happens when you push and provoke a man who has no issue disciplining insubordination," he said, sliding his thumb up a few inches and pushing it between her parted lips until it invaded her mouth and rubbed erotically against her tongue. "I've already warned you once this morning, and what you don't seem to understand is that my dick would be more than happy to provide that lesson, Bella."

She made a soft, inarticulate sound in the back of her throat, and the beat of her heart skyrocketed in her chest, but it was the ache between her legs that had her instinctively, seductively closing her lips around his thumb and grazing her teeth against the pad of his finger.

"Fuck," he groaned, his jaw clenching tight with carnal hunger as he withdrew his finger from her damp mouth and buried his fist tight in her hair instead. "Get on your knees, Bella. Right here, right now, and part those pretty lips for me."

CHAPTER NINE

ARABELLA SUCKED IN a startled breath. It wasn't a dare, or even a suggestion. His explicit words were a blatant, aggressive demand that jolted through her like a touch of electricity that was connected straight to her sex. *Oh, God,* she'd instigated this, had pushed him when she knew the repercussions because he'd made them very clear. And now she was caught in a web of her own doing and had a choice to make, and not a whole lot of time to decide judging by the impatience flashing across his features.

Even knowing she had the ability to say *no* and trusting that he'd back off and let her go, a very wanton and curious part of her wanted to please him, and she didn't question her feelings or the need to give him what he wanted. She wasn't sure what that said about her when she'd never been so brazen before, but just as she made the decision to obey, a chiming sound echoed throughout the apartment.

Maddux cursed vividly and immediately let go of her hair, though he pinned her with a stern look. "Don't fucking move."

Confusion rippled through her, but as soon as she spotted two people strolling into his penthouse from his elevator a few seconds later, she realized that with Maddux standing beside her, she at least covered his erection from the man and woman heading their way, giving him time to cool down.

Obviously, he hadn't locked out his floor from any unwanted guests or interruptions. Then again, she doubted that Maddux had intended to proposition her right there in the kitchen.

They both looked similar enough to Maddux for her to assume these two were the siblings he'd mentioned, Tempest and Hunter. Gorgeous, perfectly symmetrical features and thick dark hair ran in the family, as did those golden-brown eyes . . . which were aimed curiously at her. No sign of hostility, which led her to believe that Maddux hadn't informed his brother and sister who she was yet. She was certain the fallout wasn't going to be pretty.

"You didn't tell us you had an overnight guest," the other man said, his voice reserved as he took in the large T-shirt she still wore, which obviously belonged to Maddux. "Maybe Tempest and I should come back later to hear the details on Theodore?"

Maddux shook his head. "She isn't the kind of guest you're insinuating," he corrected his sibling, who'd pegged her as a one-night stand or something similar. Her captor exhaled a deep breath before saying, "This is Arabella Cole."

Maddux didn't beat around the bush, and that announcement changed everything. Tempest gasped in shock, and Hunter's entire body stiffened as he now glared at Arabella as if she were persona non grata, which she supposed she was. Jesus, her father had clearly done such emotional damage to all of them.

Tempest glanced from Arabella to her brother, her gaze swirling with confusion. "Maddux . . . what's going on?"

"Clearly, we need to talk," Hunter snapped heatedly before Maddux could reply.

"Yes, we do," Maddux agreed gruffly, and jerked his head toward the opposite side of the apartment. "In my office."

Maddux started in that direction, and Hunter and Tempest followed, but not before his brother shot violent daggers at her with his rage-filled gaze, and though his sister's disapproving frown wasn't nearly as threatening, Arabella definitely felt their resentment.

She remained sitting on the barstool until she heard a door close. Maddux's office must have been well insulated, because she couldn't hear anything after that, not that she wanted to be privy to whatever heated conversation the trio were about to have about her.

Not sure what to do in the meantime, she cleared their breakfast plates, did all the dishes, and cleaned the kitchen stove and countertops.

She went back to Maddux's bedroom and made the bed, then picked her ball gown off the floor to hang it up. She was nothing if not neat and orderly, and that wouldn't change just because she lived in someone else's house.

Her cell phone fell out of the pocket and hit the ground with a dull thud, and she retrieved the device, which was her only lifeline to her father. After putting her dress in the closet, she unlocked her phone to find at least a dozen calls and texts from Gavin . . . and nothing from her dad, which worried her after last night's stress and the fact that she'd had to give him one of his nitroglycerin pills to ease his chest pain.

She quickly scrolled through Gavin's messages, most of which were belligerent threats and bluster toward her captor and swearing that Maddux was going to pay for abducting her. Arabella rolled her eyes at that. She hadn't been taken hostage, not when she'd consciously offered herself to Maddux, so Gavin's claims and intimidation tactics were pointless. He just didn't like the fact that some other man had permission to touch what he'd perceived *as his*. He'd completely flip out if he knew just how much she *wanted* Maddux to do all sorts of deliciously sinful things to her.

Ignoring everything relating to Gavin, she instead called her father's number. She just needed to hear his voice and know that he was okay.

"Arabella," he answered, sounding more subdued than the self-assured parent she was used to or the spiteful man he'd been last night when confronted by Maddux. "Are you okay? Has he hurt you at all?"

"No. I'm fine, Father. I swear," she quickly assured him as she sat down on the leather bench at the foot of the bed, where Maddux had left his tuxedo, pants, and shirt from the previous evening. She'd hang those up, too. "I'm more concerned about you and your heart."

"I'm better."

She couldn't tell if he was just trying to appease her or was being truthful. "Promise me you'll go to the hospital if the pain persists." She couldn't help but fret about him since she wasn't at home to see him for herself.

"Don't worry about me. Just . . . do whatever Wilder says until I figure out how to get you out of the situation."

Sadly, she wanted to say that three million dollars was just about the only thing that would resolve the issue completely, but kept the comment to herself.

"Dad . . . how did you accumulate so much debt?" she asked, wanting to know the how and why of it all since it was such a massive amount. "Last night, there was mention that you had a gambling problem—"

"Arabella, this isn't something I want to discuss right now," he said, his voice abruptly becoming stern as he circumvented the question.

She hated that he was stonewalling her, but it didn't stop her from asking a bolder question . . . the one that *Maddux* had evaded earlier. "Okay, then what did you do to Maddux and his family to make him hate you so much?" Considering what she'd given up for her father, knowing the truth would at least help her understand why Maddux and his siblings harbored so much rage against her parent.

"It doesn't matter," her father replied in a terse tone, devastating her with his emotionless brush-off when she was currently paying the price for his debt and whatever other misdeeds he'd possibly executed. "What's done is done and you don't need to know the details. It's bad enough that Wilder has the one thing that means the most to me and will probably do everything in his power to turn you against me with false accusations and malicious lies."

As she listened to her father rant without justifying his tirade against Maddux, it occurred to Arabella that if her father was so concerned about her captor filling her head with defamatory allegations, why wasn't *he* providing the truth to give her some kind of discernable ammunition to confront Maddux with?

Because maybe her father was guilty of something really, really bad and he was attempting to twist things around to make Maddux appear the villain.

A knot of unease rose into her throat, and she swallowed hard, suddenly feeling as though her selfless actions last night had been nothing more than a reprieve for her dad that he'd taken advantage of.

So far, he'd offered no apology, no reassurances, and no explanations... and his disregard hurt when he should have been doing everything in his power to convince her of his innocence. It also left her feeling very disconnected from her father, and as though she was seeing a narcissistic, duplicitous side to him that she'd been blinded to before now.

Did she even know her father, and what his life entailed, at all?

It was a painful thought, and considering he'd managed to rack up millions in debt without her knowledge, the answer was a sobering one.

Suddenly, she had no desire to talk to him any longer, especially when she didn't know what to believe. "I need to go, Dad. I love you and I'll be in touch," she said, and disconnected the call.

Needing to distract herself, she stood up and gathered the clothing Maddux had worn last night. She draped his tuxedo jacket and slacks over her arm, and as she picked up his white dress shirt, her senses were swamped with the warm, woodsy, male fragrance that was uniquely his. She brought the material up to her nose and inhaled deeply of the testosterone-infused scent and wasn't surprised to feel desire swirl deep and low in her belly.

The arousal he'd spiked in the kitchen returned with a vengeance, and she pressed her thighs together to stave off the aching, pulsing need that Maddux was solely responsible for.

The pressure did nothing to ease the torment, and she forced herself to ignore it and headed into his enormous walk-in closet to hang up his suit. When that was done, and needing an escape, she decided that she was going to enjoy that huge soaking tub and read, which was her favorite thing to do. Losing herself in a book would guarantee to relax her and take her mind off of the reality of her situation. And if she was lucky, it would also make her forget about that unfulfilled throb between her legs.

Despite how gigantic the tub was, it filled quickly, and by the time she'd stripped out of her T-shirt and underwear and managed to put her hair up with the pins from last night, the bath was ready. She immersed herself in the steamy water, sans bubbles, and loved the fact that the tub was self-heating so the water would never get cold. Which meant she could stay right there for hours if she wanted.

After retrieving her cell phone from a nearby ledge, she opened her book app, which took her to the romance novel she'd been in the middle of reading. Except the part where she'd left off had been the start of a very explicit and erotic love scene with a hot and dominant hero, and by the time she'd finished the chapter, her own body was screaming for some kind of relief.

She was a virgin, but at age twenty-five, she'd given herself plenty of orgasms, and right now she desperately needed to take the edge off that growing lust building inside her. It certainly wouldn't take much to get the deed done.

Setting the phone back up on the shelf, she reclined in the tub, closed her eyes, and slid her hand between her legs . . . and lost herself in the fantasy of it being Maddux's long, thick fingers sliding through her folds, rubbing her sensitive clit, and providing the enticing, beckoning pleasure that was only a few strokes away.

CHAPTER TEN

MADDUX KNEW THIS conversation with his siblings was going to be difficult as hell, and as soon as they entered his penthouse office and the door closed behind Hunter and Tempest, his brother promptly unleashed his fury.

"What the fuck is going on, Maddux?" his brother snapped angrily, his eyes dark and filled with turbulent emotions. "We trusted you to stick to the plan and take down that bastard who killed our parents, and instead you decided to bring his daughter up to your penthouse so you could screw her?"

Maddux clenched his jaw, and even knowing he deserved his brother's wrath, he tried to keep his own composure collected. "I didn't screw her," he said calmly.

At least not yet, anyway. But considering what Tempest and Hunter had interrupted minutes ago, Maddux had been right on the verge of defiling Arabella's sweet, innocent mouth. The fact that she'd been two seconds away from complying with his order to get on her knees to suck his cock had made him hard enough to pound fucking nails. Discovering that Arabella had a natural submissive streak had triggered his instinct to dominate, control . . . and eventually, possess.

"What happened?" his sister asked more reasonably, her arms crossed over her chest. "Clearly, things didn't go as planned."

Maddux rubbed his fingers across his forehead, preparing himself to rehash last night's debacle. "Everything was proceeding as we'd discussed, until Theodore's daughter, Arabella, made her presence known at the door, along with the fact that she'd eavesdropped on the conversation inside the room."

Tempest frowned. "Was she aware of her father's debt or gambling problem . . . or anything else Theodore was responsible for?"

Maddux shook his head. "No, she was, and is, innocent and oblivious to her father's lifestyle and criminal activities."

Hunter dropped into one of the leather wingback chairs in the room, his long legs splayed in front of him, his expression furious. "Then maybe you should fucking tell her so she'll hate her father as much as we do."

"When the time is right, I'll make sure she knows *everything*," Maddux said, though his brother didn't look reassured.

"Okay, so Arabella overheard," Tempest said, ignoring Hunter's outburst and getting back to the conversation at hand. "That still doesn't explain why she's here and Theodore is a free man."

"He's not a free man," Maddux said, leaning his backside against his desk. "I still own him. His three-million-dollar debt and all his assets, and now, his only child and daughter, which was a deliberate and calculated choice I made."

"Really?" Hunter asked, his tone edged with disbelief.

"Yes, really," Maddux replied, giving his brother an impatient look. "Once Theodore realized he was now indebted to me, he nearly had a heart attack—"

"Too bad the fucker didn't die," Hunter interrupted bitterly.

Maddux couldn't disagree. "With her father's health at risk, it was Arabella who jumped in and begged me to take her in exchange for backing off of her father. And it was a split-second decision based on the fact that Arabella's offer nearly pushed Theodore over the edge. So, I agreed, knowing it would eat away at the old man that I had complete control over his daughter, which seemed like a nice bonus at the time."

Gripping the edge of the desk with his hands, he glanced from Hunter to Tempest, still trying to smooth things over. "Look, I *know* this wasn't the plan, but it's the way it turned out and I'm going to play the situation with Arabella by ear for now. But make no mistake. I'm not done with Theodore Cole. Not by a long shot. I'll give him a week or so of thinking the worst about Arabella living here with me, and even after I decide to give her back, I still have every intention of taking him down and exposing him for the corrupt, immoral bastard he is. I have his debt. I own every single one of his assets, and when his illegal activities come to light, his reputation and his life won't be worth shit. This doesn't change anything."

"No, it just delays it." Hunter's bitter tone came through loud and clear.

"Hunter—"

His brother held up a hand to cut off Maddux as he pushed to his feet, his gaze narrowed. "Look, you do whatever you need to do with Cole's daughter. Play your little cat-and-mouse game with her. Get her out of your goddamn system if that's the issue and then get your fucking head on straight and finish what Theodore started."

Hunter stormed out of the room, and Maddux exhaled a deep breath and rubbed a hand along his jaw, his gaze shifting to his sister, who was looking at him thoughtfully.

"Care to add anything to that?" he asked wryly.

"Sure." A small smile touched her lips. "I trust you and whatever you decide and how you decide to do it, Maddy," she said, surprisingly him with her support after his brother's tirade. "You've always taken care of us. From the day that Mom and Dad died, when you were only eighteen and Hunter and I were even younger, you've done everything in your power to keep us safe and protected. And you've worked your ass off to build a great life for all three of us," she added, indicating with a wave of her hand the warehouse he'd built into a luxurious building and apartments for each of them, and the billion-dollar security firm on the second level that provided anything and everything they could ever want or desire. "I know you want vengeance for our parents as much as Hunter and I do, and I also know that you *will* make Theodore Cole pay. The timeline has just been altered a bit. It's already been fourteen years. What's another few weeks?"

The tight, uncomfortable knot in his chest eased. "Thank you." He was grateful for those words and her understanding, despite the unexpected way things had played out.

She stepped up to him and placed a warm, affectionate hand on his forearm. "You're a good, honorable man, Maddy. If Arabella is as innocent of her father's wrongdoings as you claim, then please don't hurt her," she said, and he knew his sister wasn't referring to physical discomfort, but mental and emotional suffering. "I saw the attraction and awareness between the two of you back in the kitchen when Hunter and I arrived, which tells me she's more vulnerable in this situation than you might think or believe. It's already going to be painful enough for her when she watches her father's ugly and public downfall. She doesn't need to have her own heart shattered, too."

His sister had always been so intuitive. So tender and caring. A gentle soul . . . just like their mother. The fact that she held no resentment against Arabella just on the basis of being Theodore's daughter—unlike Hunter—said everything about her compassionate character.

But keeping Arabella here at his penthouse had nothing to do with forming an attachment or intimate emotions with her. Yes, he wanted her. Desired her. And whatever happened between them would just be about sex and pleasure, nothing more. He wasn't capable of anything beyond that. Especially with the daughter of his enemy.

"As for Hunter, he'll cool off and come around," Tempest said, an impish smile making an appearance now that all the serious conversation was off the table. "I think part of his anger and frustration toward this situation is because he met someone last night at the ball, took her back to his apartment for the night, and woke up having been ghosted. I'm sure he's feeling doubly betrayed."

Maddux winced at her choice of words but got her point. "He actually told you he had a one-night stand with someone who attended the ball?"

She nodded, her eyes bright with amusement. "Yes. On the way up here in the elevator. He was already in a mood and irritated enough about being stood up that he obviously needed to get it off his chest."

Maddux arched a brow, finding that bit of information about his brother interesting. "Since when does Hunter actually *want* more than a one and done with a woman?"

"Since last night, apparently," Tempest said cheekily. "Hunter only knows her first name, nothing else, though he said she accidentally left a bracelet behind that must have fallen off her wrist. He found it on the floor, and he's determined to track the woman down and find her. Sounds like a classic Cinderella fairy tale, doesn't it? Maybe she's *the one*." She sounded excited by the prospect.

Maddux rolled his eyes at his sister's starry-eyed, romantic notion. "Umm, no. Sorry to burst your bubble, but knowing Hunter, I'm more inclined to believe that she was a freak in the sheets and he wants a repeat." He and his brother were cut from the same cloth that way . . . dominant and completely alpha, in the boardroom *and* the bedroom.

"You are so crude, Maddy," she said, though she was laughing. "I guess we'll see, won't we? I've never seen Hunter so twisted up about a woman before, so I'd like to believe it's more than just her being a good lay."

"And what about you, baby sister?" he asked, focusing on *her* love life for a change. "Did you find *your* Prince Charming at last night's fairy-tale ball?"

A telling blush swept across her light complexion, and she averted her gaze to stare out the office windows. "No. I wasn't looking."

He smirked. "Just because you weren't looking doesn't mean you didn't get swept off your feet."

She glanced back at him, her look adorably pointed. "My feet remained firmly planted on the ground all evening long. And unlike you and Hunter, I didn't bring anyone back up to my apartment last night."

"Fair enough," he said, taking the hint to let the subject drop. "By the way, I have a favor to ask."

"Okay."

"Arabella only has her ball gown from last night," he said, not sure how his sister was going to react to the personal request that involved a woman who was still more a foe than a friend at this point. "Could she borrow something to wear until her clothing gets here this afternoon?"

"What?" Tempest gave him a feigned guileless, wide-eyed look. "You mean you don't want her prancing around your apartment all day long in your T-shirt and nothing else?"

Given the choice, he'd want Arabella naked all day long, but he kept that comment to himself. "Sarcasm doesn't become you, sister," he teased, though he couldn't blame her for her cheeky remark. "Yes or no?"

"Of course she can borrow something to wear," she said, more gracious now. "I'll bring up a pair of leggings and a blouse."

"Thank you."

He walked his sister back to the penthouse elevator, surprised to find the kitchen completely clean and Arabella nowhere in sight. He waited for Tempest to head down to her apartment and return with the clothing he'd requested, and once she'd done so and was gone again, he locked out the elevator to his floor so there would be no other random visits.

He wasn't sure where Arabella was or what she was doing, but they had unfinished business to attend to that his brother and sister had interrupted a short while ago, and Maddux had every intention of seeing just how far his sweet, virginal captive was willing to go now that they were completely alone.

CHAPTER ELEVEN

MADDUX ARRIVED IN his bedroom and realized Arabella was in his bathroom suite. He pushed open the door that hadn't been shut completely, pleased to discover her naked, soaking in the lavish tub he'd had custom made for himself. Of all the scenarios in his head of how Arabella was passing time, he never would have imagined this one. Not that he was disappointed in the least.

He was also immediately aware that while her eyes were closed, she wasn't asleep—not according to the gentle rippling of water across the surface of the bath that lapped against her upper chest, indicating she was indulging in another form of activity. Her hand was clearly moving beneath the water—between her legs by his estimation—and she must have hit an especially sensitive spot as her head lolled along the rim of the tub, her lips parted, and a soft moan tumbled out.

Heat and a primitive hunger coursed through his blood, lengthening his cock beneath the front placket of his jeans until he felt as though he might burst through the denim. He was pleasantly surprised to know that she was attuned to her body and had no qualms about enjoying her own pleasure. Except, for as seductive as this image in front of him was, there was no fucking way he was going to let her finish what he'd initiated out in the kitchen earlier.

If anyone satisfied her need to come, it would be him.

Feet still bare from getting out of bed this morning, he crossed the bathroom into the larger spa area in stealth mode. Her increasingly panting breaths, her beautifully flushed face, and the quickening pace of her fingers dancing across her clit told him she was close to orgasm. Finally reaching her, he bent down, dipped his hand into the clear water, and encircled her wrist with his fingers, jerking her hand away from her pussy.

Her lashes flew open, a startled squeak escaped her throat, and her body jerked upright, sloshing water over the rim of the tub and soaking the front of his jeans. Her shocked, wide-eyed gaze stared up at his face, and he knew she clearly saw his fierce, deliberately displeased expression.

"Maddux." Her voice wavered as she uttered his name, and her cheeks pinkened even more with embarrassment at being caught in the act.

"Bella." His tone was dark and as dominant as the urges she brought out in him, and he did nothing to soften or hide those aggressive tendencies. "Such a naughty girl," he murmured, caressing his thumb along the rapid pulse beating in the wrist he still held. "I leave you alone for a short while, and you think it's okay to slide your fingers into your pussy and make yourself come?"

Her tongue licked nervously across her bottom lip, which didn't help the fact that his dick was throbbing relentlessly. "I . . . umm . . . didn't think you'd walk in here," she said in a rush.

"Why wouldn't I?" he refuted with an arch of his brow. "Last I checked, this was my bathroom, my shower, and my tub. I don't need permission to come into any of the rooms in my apartment, so don't ever assume I won't seek you out at any given time. You gave up your right to complete privacy when you agreed to give yourself over to me and then stepped off the elevator into my penthouse."

Much to his surprise, her chin tipped up with the slightest show of stubborn attitude. "Okay. Good to know."

She hadn't argued, but the fact that her voice held just a small trace of mockery was enough to provoke him further. "Here's another rule for you to obey while you live here," he said, establishing who, exactly, was in control. "Your orgasms are now *mine* to give, when and *if* I feel as though you deserve them. From this moment forward, getting yourself off without my permission will be a punishable offense. If I ever catch you finger fucking yourself again without me in the room, I will tease and torment your clit until you're begging for release, but instead of letting you come, I will keep you in orgasm denial, which, if you're not familiar with the term for that particular kink, is called edging. Trust me, Bella, I will enjoy the punishment. *You* will not, so don't test me."

"Okay," she said, this time in a softer, more subdued tone.

Satisfied with her acquiescence, he released her hand, stood up, and began unbuttoning his jeans. Which wasn't an easy feat over his hard-as-steel erection. When his pants were finally open, he slid his thumbs into the waistband of his jeans and briefs to shove them down his hips.

"What are you doing?" she asked in a breathless, nervous rush.

He stilled. God, she was such a paradox, which was truly one of the things that drew him to her. Bold and mouthy one moment and blushing and adorably bashful the next. "I'm in the mood for a bath," he told her.

"Okay, I'll leave, and you can have the bathroom to yourself," she insisted, averting her gaze.

When she put her hands on the edge of the tub to push herself to her feet, he immediately stopped her. "No, you will stay right where you are because I'm going to join you." The fact that she complied and sank back down into the water shot a nice little rush of sexual adrenaline through him.

"And you *will* watch me undress, Bella, so you see how hard you make me," he ordered when she kept her eyes focused straight ahead and not at him. "Look at me." His tone was low and commanding.

Shockingly enough, she didn't defy him and turned her head. But instead of fixating her stare at the open fly of his jeans, where he wanted it to be, her eyes lifted up to his face. The corner of his mouth twitched at her impertinence, and he had to consciously tamp down the amused grin tugging at his lips.

Technically, she *was* looking at him, and he knew her choice to avoid his dick was a deliberate and sly decision . . . all without disobeying him. Clearly, if there was a loophole in his request, then his Bella was going to find and take advantage of it.

"Aim those eyes about three feet lower, sweetheart," he instructed in a silky murmur. "I want you to get used to seeing and feeling the size of my cock in your hands before I decide to bury every single inch in your tight pussy or your mouth, like would have happened earlier if my brother and sister hadn't arrived just in time." When she didn't immediately comply, he said, "I won't ask you again. Look *down*." He wasn't stripping out of his jeans and briefs until he had her full attention there.

Her lips pursed, but again, she obeyed. Except, instead of a quick drop to his midsection, the minx decided to take a slow, leisurely trip downward, her gaze taking in the width of his shoulders, his defined chest, and the abs that disappeared into the waistband of his black underwear. Beneath the tight, clinging fabric of his boxer briefs, the thick length of his erection was prominently displayed, leaving no question of just how well-endowed he was.

He waited for signs of trepidation from her but saw none. If anything, curiosity and anticipation etched her features.

"Have you seen a naked man before?" Just because she hadn't been fucked didn't mean she hadn't done other intimate things with a guy.

"Yes. Of course." She drew her legs up and wrapped her arms around her knees, covering herself and making room for him at the other end of the tub. "In pictures and videos I've seen on the internet and Tumblr," she admitted, which was a virtual porn haven, so yeah, he had no doubt she'd eyed a few boners.

"Good," he said, sliding down his pants and briefs a few inches before adding in a droll tone, "So you won't faint at the sight of my dick then."

She huffed out a small laugh. "Doubtful. I'm a virgin, Maddux. Not a nun or a prude. Don't be shocked, but I even have a vibrator at home that looks and feels like the real deal."

Ahh, Jesus. He swallowed a groan, the filthy thought of her fucking a dildo and coming all over it making him hot as hell. Without any other hesitations, he shoved his jeans and underwear down his legs, and once he had them off, he tossed them onto the floor in a dry area of the bathroom before turning back to face her. "You'll have to let me know how that vibrator compares to my dick when the time comes and you're impaled on my cock."

Somehow, she feigned a neutral expression as she stared at his jutting shaft. "Hmmm. I think you're a few inches smaller, actually."

He couldn't hold back the deep laughter that erupted from his chest at her bluff and stroked his engorged flesh, even *his* big hand was barely able to grip it all. "Tell me that when I've got all nine thick inches stretching you full and keeping you pinned to my mattress as I fuck you so hard and deep you'll be sore for days, Bella. I sincerely doubt your vibrator can compare to that."

She had no sassy retort to that as he stepped into the tub opposite of where she was sitting. The water was still nice and hot thanks to the built-in heater and rose to the rim with his weight as he sank down to a comfortable reclining position.

"How did your conversation with your brother and sister go?" she asked curiously.

She was surprisingly comfortable with him naked in the tub with her. Another contradiction, he mused, as he shrugged at her question. "As good as it could have gone considering what they'd expected to happen last night. My brother is pissed that you're here when your father should have been on his knees last night begging for leniency," he said honestly. "But Tempest is more... empathetic about the situation. If you need anything and I'm not around or you can't get ahold of me, she will assist you."

"Thank you. That's good to know." She absently swirled her hands in the water, her gaze suddenly turning serious as it met his. "I... umm... want you to know up front that I called and talked to my father."

He liked that she didn't keep that secret from him. It went a long way in building trust with him. "Anything you'd like to share?"

She shook her head. "No. He avoided my questions about the debt he'd accumulated and I had no clue about... and when I asked about why you hated him so much, he said I didn't need to know the details, which is annoying as hell since neither one of you will enlighten me."

He ran his wet fingers through his long hair, pushing it away from his face. "Of course he doesn't want you to know the details, because revealing the truth would be equivalent to him admitting guilt."

"Guilt for *what*?" she persisted.

It would be so easy to divulge what an unscrupulous man her father was, as well as Gavin's part in it all. But knowing that the cold, hard facts would crush someone as good-hearted and kind as Arabella, he didn't answer her question. He wasn't ready to deal with the emotional upheaval that would accompany such a shocking bombshell. Not yet, anyway. He swore when the timing was right, when discovering the truth had the most impact, she'd learn what a fucking scumbag Theodore Cole was.

But right now, he didn't want to discuss his hatred toward her father, not when Maddux wanted his hands all over this woman... and more specifically, giving her that orgasm he'd interrupted when he'd walked in on her earlier.

"Come over to my side of the tub, Bella," he ordered, effectively changing the mood between them to something more seductive. "Sit between my spread legs, facing away from me."

She blinked at him in surprise at the abrupt change in conversation and licked her bottom lip. "Why?"

"Because I said so," he replied bluntly. "Because I want to show you exactly what your body is capable of feeling when it's *my* hands and fingers delivering the pleasure."

Her chin tipped up a fraction, a daring light glimmering in her eyes. "And if I say no?"

She was testing him... and it occurred to Maddux that she enjoyed the *cat-and-mouse* game his brother had alluded to earlier. The tempting. The teasing. And the anticipation of waiting and seeing what he'd say or how he'd react to her willful attitude.

She had no idea what kind of perverse opponent he truly was. "Defy me, and that orgasm you were about to give yourself before I stopped it will leave you aching for the rest of the day, and night, since I forbid you to touch yourself." He casually rested his arms along the wide rim of the tub. "Obey, and I'll make you come so good and so hard you'll be addicted to my touch."

A cheeky smile flirted at the edges of her lush, kissable mouth. "You think very highly of yourself, Mr. Wilder."

"Come here, Bella," he said on a low, impatient growl. "*Now.*"

No hesitation or argument this time, giving credence to the fact that she liked his bossy, dominant side. Good thing, considering what he planned to do to her.

She moved toward him, the depth of the water covering up to her chest, though he enjoyed a glimpse of her rosy nipples beneath the surface before she turned and settled between his widespread thighs, just as he'd instructed, but of course deliberately keeping too much distance between them.

Her startled gasp echoed in the bathroom as he took hold of her tiny waist and guided her back farther, until her posterior was tucked right up against his groin and his rigid cock nestled in that soft crease in between her ass cheeks, which felt so fucking good.

"Lie back against my chest and make yourself comfortable," he told her.

He heard her exhale a deep breath. "Easier said than done when there's a nine-inch spike prodding me in the back."

He chuckled, feeling a tad bit smug. "Ahhh, doesn't feel so small now, does it, Bella?"

"No," she whispered as she reclined.

Her petite height came up short when aligned against his longer torso, and he lifted her a few inches higher so her head was able to rest on his shoulder, and she was now sitting on his lap, giving his arms and hands better reach to intimate places, as well.

She squirmed restlessly against his dick. "I . . . umm, fibbed about the size of my vibrator and I'd be lying if I didn't admit that the size of your erection makes me . . . nervous. I'm not sure how you're going to fit."

She sounded genuinely concerned, and he sought to reassure her, which wasn't his normal approach with women. Then again, Arabella's inexperience was new to him, too.

"I'm not fucking you today, so you can relax for now," he said, sliding his hands along her flat stomach, letting her get used to his touch. "But when I do, I can promise that I'll make sure your pussy is nice and slick and ready to accommodate my width and length. I won't take you like a battering ram, if that's your worry," he added in a lighter, teasing tone.

She laughed softly, and the last bit of tension seemed to ease away as her body yielded against his, light and weightless in the water. "Now there's an image I'd rather not have in my head, thank you very much," she said, her voice wry.

"Then let's find something more enjoyable for you to focus on," he murmured seductively, and proceeded to do just that.

CHAPTER TWELVE

EXCITEMENT SHIFTED THROUGH Arabella as Maddux didn't hesitate to do what he did best and took control. Before she realized his intent, he hooked his feet along the insides of her ankles and used that leverage to spread her legs wide and keep them pinned against the sides of the tub. Then he took her arms and folded them behind her back, with her palms flat against his chest between them, effectively immobilizing all her limbs.

She didn't protest or struggle, but she knew the quickening of her breath told Maddux how aroused she already was by her restrained and exposed position. Once again, he splayed both of his palms on her belly, then simultaneously swept one hand up toward her chest until he captured the firm mound of one breast while the other slid down between her legs, his fingers stroking along the outer folds of her pussy, avoiding her clit and teasing her sensitive flesh with soft, light strokes.

"*Maddux*," she moaned, trying to lift her hips to deepen the pressure of his touch, but with her legs held open by the strength of his, she could only manage to squirm restlessly.

He turned his head and nuzzled his warm lips against the side of her neck, the light growth of beard on his face abrading her skin and adding another level of pleasure she didn't think was possible. "Something you want, Bella?" he taunted, nipping on her ear as he pulled on her taut nipple, lightly twisted, then pinched the hard nub of flesh, sending sparks of conflicting sensations rippling through her body.

She cried out as that sting of blissful pain spiraled straight down to her throbbing core, where his fingers rubbed and swirled against her clit. "Yes, please," she begged, panting, already desperate for relief. "Make me come."

She felt him smile against her cheek, clearly enjoying having the upper hand. "Not yet. But soon."

His strumming fingers backed off a fraction, leaving her bereft and teetering on the edge. In retaliation, she did the only thing she could think of... she gyrated back on his cock, stoking the length of his shaft between the cheeks of her ass—which increased her own desire, too.

"Fuck," he growled, instinctively thrusting his hips along that crevice as he shoved two fingers deep inside her in his own form of punishment, making the water ripple violently around them.

She gasped in shock, feeling her body clamp down on those digits as he slowly withdrew them, then pushed in again, stretching and filling her while his thumb massaged her clit until the ache between her legs became a relentless, needy throb that he refused to appease.

She tried to thrash, and her hands he'd positioned behind her back dug into his stomach. Without thinking of the consequences, she raked and scraped her nails across his skin like a wildcat, hard enough to scratch and make him hiss out a harsh breath.

The fingers tweaking her nipples abruptly came up and wrapped around her throat beneath her chin, pulling her head back against his shoulder until she was forced to arch her spine to accommodate the position since her legs were still locked down by his. If she thought she was restrained before, now she was totally at his mercy, and the realization jolted her with a rush of forbidden, thrilling pleasure that only added to the knot of lust coiling tighter and tighter inside her.

His breathing was harsh and damp against her neck. "Jesus Christ, who knew you were such a filthy fucking girl who liked to fight dirty?" he mused, dark amusement threading his voice. "You like the struggle, don't you? But mostly, you like *this* part. Where you fight and I dominate and control and *take*."

She did . . . Oh, God, *she did*. Her skin flushed hotly, and a whimpering sound escaped from her throat at the thought of him doing dirty, wicked, shameless things to her body. She'd had no idea that such depraved behavior could turn her on so much, that a man's sexually aggressive nature could make her submit willingly just to experience such power and immense pleasure.

But *this man* made her want it all.

"Make no mistake, Bella," he went on in a silky-smooth voice as the fingers between her legs began dancing across her sensitive clit again in slow, torturous circles, and he turned her head just slightly so he could look at her face, though his hand remained anchored around her throat. "I could *take* you just like this, but I promised you I wouldn't. Under normal circumstances, your little act of rebellion would earn you the flat of my hand against your tender ass, but I'm feeling benevolent *this* time . . . and selfishly, I want to watch you come for me. It isn't going to take much, is it?"

The way his hand pressed firmly against her jaw, she couldn't shake her head in answer. But yes, she was so ramped up that, with every illicit caress he made against that hard, aching nub of flesh, the monstrous need grew, so swift and so strong her entire body began to shake with the force of the orgasm threatening to overwhelm her.

He eased his hold on her chin, let his fingers relax from around her throat as the peak of rapture spilled through her veins. All the while he kept his dark, hot gaze on her face, watching every nuance, every reaction, his own expression etched with a lust and hunger that escalated her ecstasy. Her eyes rolled back, and her lips parted on a soft cry as her climax engulfed her utterly and completely, unlike anything her body had ever experienced before.

He only gave her a few extra seconds to come down from the high before he released her legs, then flipped her around so that she was facing him. He grabbed the backs of her thighs in his hands and jerked her upward so that she was straddling his legs and his erection jutted between them beneath the surface of the water.

"Put your hands on my cock," he ordered, his voice a hoarse, desperate rasp of sound as he plowed all ten fingers into her hair,. knocking the pins from the upswept strands as he brought her face closer to his, the color of his eyes like molten gold. "Wrap all ten fingers around me and stroke my dick, nice and tight, from the base all the way up to the head."

Wanting to please him more than she wanted her next breath, she did everything he asked, at first awkwardly. She might have seen penises in pictures and online, but this was the first time she'd ever held one in her hands, and he was huge. But she managed to find a rhythm that made him groan like a dying man, and with his hands framing her face, he brought her mouth to his in a deeply searing kiss. She immediately opened to the hungry thrust of his tongue, savoring the dark, intoxicating flavor that was uniquely his, while trying her best to keep her grip on his shaft as tight as possible as his hips started to thrust erratically, his cock jackhammering between the pressure and friction of her palms.

He seemed to grow harder and thicker in her hands, if that was even possible. Then he was growling roughly against her lips, his body stiffening, his tongue delving deeper into her mouth as he gasped and grunted, his muscles tensing as he embraced his own orgasm. He tore his mouth from hers, let his head drop back against the rim of the tub as a hoarse, animal-like sound rose from his chest, then broke free from his throat.

His control seemed to shatter. Dirty, filthy, obscene words fell from his lips, and his hands released her hair and gripped the porcelain ledge, as if he needed the anchor as his hips jerked and his body shuddered. Against her clasped palms, she felt a pulsing sensation like a volatile heartbeat and glanced down to where she was still stroking him with both hands, watching in pure fascination as a thick stream of hot, slick fluid erupted from the engorged head with each subsequent throb of the bulging vein that ran beneath the length of his erection.

She'd never seen anything as hot, wild, or primitive as Maddux in the throes of pleasure, and even after, when he tried to catch his breath. As she tentatively, experimentally squeezed the flushed, swollen tip of his shaft and caressed her thumb over that plump flesh, his hips flexed and he cursed, grabbing both her hands beneath the water and yanking them away from his still-hard flesh.

"Trust me, vixen, there's not a drop of come left in me after that release," he said, his thumbs rubbing the insides of her wrists as he placed her hands on his chest. "Just like your clit is sensitive after an orgasm, my dick is, too."

She had no idea, and she couldn't deny that everything about his body enthralled her and made her want to learn more. She lifted her gaze to Maddux's, his expression more relaxed than she'd seen it since they'd met, and a part of her recognized that *she* was responsible for that calm, satisfied look on his face.

The realization was a heady one. As was the awareness that she'd had the ability to strip away all that power and control he wore like a shield and had reduced him to just a man responding to her touch and the pleasure she'd given him.

She licked her bottom lip, and his heavy-lidded gaze tracked the glide of her tongue. "That was . . . incredible. *You're* incredible," she added, and though that second sentence had been spontaneous, it was the truth.

Those honest words caused something intimate and unexpected to shift between them. There was no denying Maddux was a complex man with deeply rooted anger because of her father's actions, along with a brash attitude meant to keep him from forming close relationships outside of his siblings, and with *her* specifically. But with his defenses lowered like this, she was beginning to suspect that his brusque demeanor was his way of camouflaging the real and varying range of his emotions that showed a caring, humane, and compassionate side to his personality. One he didn't like on display, as was evident in the way his mercurial mood shifted once again and his placid features hardened over.

An almost cruel smile twisted his lips. "Don't mistake sexual gratification for anything more from me," he said, shattering the harmonious moment between them. "Because I guarantee if you romanticize this arrangement, you'll be disillusioned and sorely disappointed when it ends."

With that, he abruptly stood up, sloshing water all over the place and forcing Arabella to move to the other side of the tub to give him the room he clearly wanted and needed. Beyond being modest with him, she brazenly took in the sight of him . . . magnificently naked and dripping wet, with rivulets of water mapping a course down his beautifully honed body.

He grabbed a large towel off the heating rack and wrapped it around his waist, not looking at her. "My sister brought up some things for you to wear until your clothes arrive, and I have work I need to do, so I'll be in my office and don't want to be disturbed unless it's an emergency."

He walked out of the bathroom, dismissing her. Clearly, escaping to his office was Maddux's way of shutting her out, and Arabella would be a bald-faced liar if she said that his disregard didn't hurt after what they'd just shared. Then again, she supposed their mutual pleasure had provided a far more intimate connection for her than for an experienced man like Maddux, who was no doubt used to sexually sophisticated women who didn't *romanticize* their encounters with him.

But even knowing that, she didn't regret what had just happened, not when everything about his confident control had awakened those illicit desires she'd always harbored deep inside. It was as though he'd put a match to a flame, and she'd do anything to please him, already knowing her submission, just like she'd offered a short while ago, would ultimately be rewarded with the sweetest ecstasy.

For the most part, she'd remained a virgin because no man had ever come close to arousing her mind and body the way Maddux just had, and she'd always known that sweet and gentle and considerate sex didn't appeal to her. No, the images that filled her mind while masturbating had always featured a dark, edgy, sexually assertive man who dominated all her senses. She'd always believed her fantasies were depraved and taboo and perverse . . . until now, with Maddux.

It was as though she'd been waiting for the right man to come along, who knew exactly what her body craved and how to indulge those shameless needs she'd only entertained in her head.

But never, even in her wildest dreams, would she believe that man would come in the form of one who only wanted her for revenge.

CHAPTER THIRTEEN

MADDUX HAD NO idea when he'd grown a conscience as far as his plans for retribution against Theodore went. After years of devising the other man's ruin, he'd allowed a woman to fuck everything up. Taking Arabella in exchange for Theodore had been a spontaneous choice and a huge mistake, and that was even more clear to him after his tryst with her in the bathtub.

He didn't expect someone as sweet and guileless as Arabella to be so uninhibited... or that she'd enjoy his brand of sexual dominance. Even as a virgin, and despite her sass and stubborn attitude, it was clear that she was a submissive creature who liked being restrained and forced to cede her pleasure to him. And Jesus Christ, she'd been so fucking perfect and beautiful when he'd finally allowed her to come, and even more stunning when she obeyed his order to get him off right after that. She might have been inexperienced when it came to jerking a man off, but she'd been an eager and devoted learner, and he'd been so fucking helpless to resist her zealous attempts.

But it was the aftermath of that encounter and the soft, starry-eyed way she'd looked up at him that had delivered a hard and much needed jolt of reality to what had just happened. Especially when his sister's earlier warning about Arabella being vulnerable in this situation, and to Maddux's intentions, added to the turmoil swirling inside him.

He exhaled on an irritable growl and spun his leather chair around to look out the office windows instead of staring at his computer screen, because his concentration at the moment was shit anyway.

When had he become such an unscrupulous, apathetic asshole that he'd take an innocent woman and use her as a pawn in this dangerous game with Theodore? When he'd accepted her proposition, it had been on the premise of making her father, and Gavin, suffer. Knowing that Arabella was under his command and thinking the worst of her situation and letting that knowledge eat them both up inside.

Yes, he'd initially intended to corrupt Arabella as part of his plan and send her back to her father after stripping her of her innocence, but after what had happened between them in the bathroom, he'd felt an unpredicted emotional shift inside of him. Especially when it occurred to him that Arabella would have willingly surrendered her body and her virtue to him if he'd wanted to fuck her. No questions asked.

In an unusual flash of integrity, he'd realized that her virginity wasn't his to steal on the basis of anger and resentment toward another person. He didn't have it in him to destroy her or defile her, and he couldn't take something so significant that didn't belong to him, no matter how badly he wanted to be the first and only man to possess her so completely. He was far from being a man worthy of that offering, and he certainly had nothing substantial to give a kindhearted woman like Arabella in return. He didn't do love, and he most definitely didn't believe in happily ever afters.

Bottom line, Arabella had no hand in his parents' deaths and her only misfortune was having been sired by an evil, unethical man. Maddux refused to break her spirit or crush her self-esteem. Holding her captive wasn't about what his dick wanted. It was all about psychological warfare against Theodore, but even with that understanding, Maddux wondered if the other man was really concerned about his daughter's welfare at this point, or more relieved that he wasn't currently in jeopardy of having his entire life implode. Arabella had selflessly given him that reprieve.

Maddux rubbed a weary hand along his jaw, deciding he'd keep Arabella a week—while doing his best to avoid her and the temptation she'd presented—which would give him time to formulate what move he wanted and needed to make next.

The chiming sound of the elevator approaching his penthouse pulled Maddux out of his thoughts, and he swiveled his chair back to his desk and switched on his security monitor to oversee the delivery of Arabella's personal items. He'd received a text a short while ago that Milo and Cooper, two of his trusted security guys, were on their way back from Theodore's with what they were able to collect.

Surprisingly, as they'd told him via text message, Theodore hadn't resisted or given his men any flack about gathering his daughter's clothing and toiletries. The man's passive demeanor was another thing that led Maddux to believe that Arabella's father was taking advantage of his respite, at his daughter's expense.

A few seconds later, both Milo and Cooper stepped from the elevator, each of them rolling two suitcases. One of the many security cameras in his apartment showed Arabella, wearing the black leggings and blouse Tempest had lent her, in his bedroom. At the sound of the elevator, she'd walked into the living room to see who'd arrived. Because his security system had audio, he turned up the volume and was able to listen to their conversation, which mainly consisted of Arabella politely thanking his men for delivering her things.

Once they were gone, Maddux should have

switched off the monitor, but instead he leaned back in the chair and watched Arabella put away her clothing in his closet and her toiletries in his bathroom, mixing her feminine stuff with his masculine items when he'd never before had a woman's things cluttering up his vanity. When all that was done, she grabbed a small computer tablet, made herself comfortable on his living room couch, and started to read.

Again, Maddux could have shut down the feed, but even as he brought up work emails on his computer to go through, he kept the security monitor on Arabella. A few hours passed as she lost herself in her book, then fell asleep . . . and even though she was essentially doing nothing but relaxing all afternoon, he found himself enjoying watching her way too much.

She woke up and stretched languidly, his unruly dick stirring at the soft, sexy groaning noise she made as she elongated her limbs. She stood up, her head tipping curiously to the side as she peered up at one of the small cameras mounted in the corner of the room. She moved closer to it, an amused smile curving her lips as she stared straight into the lens . . . and essentially, straight at him.

"I'm assuming this is a fancy security system considering what you do for a living," she said, talking to him as if he was in the room with her. "And that little red light is probably on because you're watching and listening to me, which isn't fair because I can't see you," she added with a cute little pout. "As I'm sure you saw, it's been an incredibly boring Sunday afternoon, and I hope you're getting a ton of work done locked up in your office. I have strict orders not to bother you ... but I am kind of curious what would happen if I deliberately ignored your growly, grouchy demand and was a bit of a nuisance while you worked."

Her big blue eyes filled with mischief as she thoughtfully tapped a finger against her chin. "I'm thinking maybe I'd deserve one of those spankings you mentioned, for being so defiant."

A low, heated growl rose up from his chest and tightened his cock at the brazen suggestion, along with the way she so ingenuously blinked her lashes up at him when she knew exactly what she was saying and doing. She was fearlessly goading him, and his goddamn palm itched to show her just how good and arousing that punishment could feel.

As difficult as it was, he tamped down the urge to walk out into the living room, bend her over the back of the couch, pull down her pants, and call her bluff. But he'd just vowed to keep his distance from Arabella, and his hands off her, and if his palm so much as made contact with her bare ass, it wouldn't stop at one playful swat. No, it would end with her moaning for more and his fingers sliding deep inside her drenched pussy.

A soft little sigh slipped past her lips and

reached his ears through the speakers. "You know, even though I'm tempted to interrupt you while you're working, I'm going to be a good girl and behave, even if I'm coming to realize that it is way more fun being bad." She delivered that with a naughty smile. "By the way, I'm starved and I'm going to make something for dinner, just in case you're hungry and you want to join me and have some friendly conversation."

She waited a handful of seconds, staring up at the camera expectantly, as if waiting for him to answer . . . then spoke again. "Hmm. I'll take it by your silence that's a no," she said, her tone light and teasing.

She was so adorable she made him fucking laugh. A genuine chuckle that was rare for him. The speaker wasn't two-way, so he couldn't have answered anyway, but just the fact that she was carrying on this ridiculous and amusing one-way conversation with herself had him unable to turn off the monitor or look away. He didn't want to miss a thing.

Leaving the living room, she sauntered into the kitchen, and as soon as she spied the camera pointed in that direction, she grinned and waved at him. "Hey, it's you again!" she said gregariously, even though she couldn't have been one hundred percent certain he was watching her. "So, let's see what I have to work with for dinner."

She opened the refrigerator and peered inside. "Since you're not here to tell me what I can and can't use, everything is game as far as I'm concerned."

She pulled out a carton of heavy whipping cream, a flat of fresh mushrooms, an onion, garlic, and butter. Then she started searching through his cupboards, adding a can of chicken broth to those items, a container of flour, and some spices. And then she proceeded to entertain him as she made fresh cream of mushroom soup from scratch, while providing hilarious commentary as she cut the onion and garlic and stirred in all the ingredients.

When the soup thickened and steam rose from the pot, she took a deep breath of the scent, closed her eyes, and moaned in pure pleasure. She glanced up at the camera, smiling. "I know you're probably a meat-and-potatoes kind of guy, but this is going to be delicious with the garlic toast I'm making and you're missing out."

His stomach growled hungrily, echoing Arabella's sentiment as she ladled the soup into a bowl, retrieved the garlic toast from the oven, and sat down with her meal at the counter, facing the camera. The impulse to join her was overwhelmingly strong . . . not just for the food, but to enjoy her company in person. The past hour of watching her, listening to her joke and tease despite the less-than-ideal circumstances he'd put her in made his respect for her grow exponentially.

He *wanted* to spend time with her—an anomaly for him when it came to women in general—but he was smart enough to know that sitting beside Arabella while they shared dinner was just as tempting and dangerous as touching her.

But that didn't stop her from continuing her one-sided conversation with him, or Maddux from listening.

She lifted a spoonful of soup to her pursed lips and blew on the hot liquid before taking the bite, her gaze lifting back up to the camera. "I don't know how much you know about me. I'm sure a security guy like you can find out anything on anyone at the snap of your fingers, and considering who I am, I'm sure you have a file full of information on me," she said wryly.

Yes, he did. Right in the desk drawer next to where he was sitting. But somehow, Maddux suspected he was about to get a more intimate insight to Arabella Cole, and all his attention was focused on her.

"But from my personal account, and not from some impersonal private investigator's perspective, my life in general has been fairly boring, predictable and . . . lonely." Her voice dropped to a more somber tone as she absently dipped her bread into her soup. "My mother died when I was five, and even though I knew my father cared about me, he mostly showed it in tangible things that didn't really matter to me. Not when I wanted his attention the most. But I suppose he didn't really know what to do with a little girl, and

I'd like to think he did the best he could, given the circumstances."

Maddux refused to feel any kind of empathy toward Theodore, but he couldn't deny the compassion he felt toward Arabella. He knew what it was like to lose a parent, the void it left, and the pain that might have dulled over time but still existed. The fact that they'd shared that same experience, even if their parents' deaths had been vastly different, softened something inside of him.

"I think it was just easier for him to enroll me in an all-girls boarding school so he didn't have to worry about me, but I hated feeling so sheltered and confined. And I was scared a lot of the time, too, so I'd go to the school library and find a quiet corner and read for hours after class and on the weekends." A small smile touched the corner of her mouth as she swallowed a spoonful of soup. "I've always been an introvert, because it was much easier and safer to just stay in my own little bubble. I always had my nose in a book, and I loved all the classics. Jane Austen, Charlotte Bronte, Nathaniel Hawthorne. The characters in those books were like my best friends."

She pushed her spoon through the remnants of her soup, seemingly lost in thought. "It's really no surprise that I focused on a degree in English literature in college, then went on to get my master's in library science. And now, I work at the university library as a digital data analyst and curator. I know it doesn't *sound* exciting, but I really love my job . . . I just wish I felt the same way about other aspects of my life," she said, so quietly he had to strain to hear her.

"But . . . I'm trying to change that," she said, injecting an upbeat tone to her voice. "I'm asserting myself more instead of letting my father or Gavin dictate what I should do or how I should act, and that feels really good." She lifted her gaze back up to the camera, an impish grin on her lips. "Believe it or not, I wasn't always rebellious or stubborn or sassy. But I like the new and improved me . . . and I think you like it, too."

Yeah, he did, he thought with a smile. He liked it, and her, way too much.

She set her spoon in her empty bowl and rested her arms on the counter, her expression soft and beautiful and honest. "I just want you to know, I have no regrets about what I did last night. Not because I saved my father . . . because I'm starting to believe that I don't know my father all that well . . . but because you, Maddux Wilder, are the most exciting, thrilling adventure I've ever experienced, and I'm not sure I want it to end anytime soon."

That statement, so genuine and pure, stole his breath and wreaked havoc with Maddux's goddamn emotions, filling him with feelings he'd thought were dead and buried and impossible to resurrect. He didn't want to care about Arabella, but he couldn't deny that she'd cracked something open inside of him and it was already happening.

The pull toward her, the growing connection, was undeniable, and it scared the fuck out of him because he didn't do emotions, and more importantly, they had no chance at a future together. Not once he let her go, and not after he devastated her father's life.

Then there would only be hatred. Which was why he had to keep his distance.

CHAPTER FOURTEEN

THE NEXT MORNING, Arabella woke up in Maddux's bed alone, and she couldn't ignore the twist of disappointment at that discovery. But as she glanced over at the empty space beside hers, finding the covers and his pillow still neat and orderly, she realized that he must have slept elsewhere. So yes, she was bummed, but she couldn't say she was surprised. Not after the way he'd holed himself up in his office all night long in his attempt to ignore her.

Refusing to start the day being mopey over something that was beyond her control, she got out of bed and headed right for the camera mounted in the corner of the bedroom, red light on. He had the ability to spy on her from every angle in the apartment, and she could only assume that he was watching her.

Uncaring that her hair was a tangled mess and she probably looked completely rumpled, she put her hands on her hips and looked up at the lens. "Good morning, Maddux," she said cheerfully. "You know, you could have slept in your own bed last night. I would have behaved and kept my hands to myself, if that was your concern. I swear I wouldn't have taken advantage of you or your incredible body. At least, not unless you wanted me to." She grinned cheekily.

The one thing she'd learned while cooking dinner by herself and talking to Maddux via the security cameras the evening before was that speaking to an inanimate object gave her a sense of freedom to be open and honest without having to worry about couching her words or thoughts, which was why she'd been so candid when talking about her childhood and her life in general last night. Because she wanted Maddux to know the *real* Arabella Cole, who was more than just Theodore's daughter. The woman with goals and hopes and dreams. The woman with needs and desires and fantasies she wanted to explore with him. She'd been truthful when she'd confessed that he was the most exciting, thrilling adventure she'd ever experienced.

Speaking to Maddux through the camera meant he wasn't there in person to turn hot and cold on a dime or give her an annoyed scowl if she said something he didn't like . . . or walk away when their attraction came to a head. It offered her the ability to break down his barriers, with no argument or dismissive attitude from him.

"So, what is the second hardest thing in the morning?" she asked, just to inject some humor into the beginning of the day and be a little naughty with him. She let a few seconds pass before delivering the punch line. "Getting up!"

She laughed at her own joke and imagined him groaning at the silly pun. "I know that was really cheesy, but it was off the top of my head and spur-of-the-moment and the best I could do. I promise to brush up on my one-liners."

Leaving him on that note, she walked into the bathroom and shut the door, and at least she had privacy in there as she used the facilities, brushed her teeth, did her hair and makeup, and got ready for her workday. Once she was changed into a dress and heels, she grabbed her phone from where it was charging on the nightstand and headed into the kitchen.

She poured herself a cup of coffee from the carafe that Maddux must have left heating for her, then found a piece of paper with a scrawled note on it. *I made you an omelet for breakfast. It's in the refrigerator and you just need to heat it up in the microwave.* He'd signed the message with a bold *M*.

The fact that he'd thought about her in any capacity made Arabella ridiculously happy. She glanced up at the security camera pointing toward the kitchen and smiled. "Thank you, Maddux. That was incredibly sweet of you." She'd deliberately used the word *sweet*, just because she knew it would probably annoy him, when he undoubtedly thought of himself as anything but that.

As she warmed up what looked to be a yummy and fluffy ham and cheese omelet, she scrolled through her text messages . . . discovering at least another dozen new ones from Gavin since yesterday, which she ignored like all the rest. And damn, it felt good not to have to answer to him for anything.

She was surprised to find a different message with the name Maddux attached to it, which read, *Milo is driving you to work this morning and will be your security detail for the day. He'll meet you on the first floor at 7:30 a.m.*

She blinked at the message, realizing that at some point Maddux had to have come into the room while she'd been sleeping to text himself her number from her cell phone, which enabled her to reach him in return.

She couldn't resist provoking him. *Will I get in trouble if I ditch him?*

Try it and see, came his quick reply.

She leaned against the counter, grinning as she typed out another teasing retort. *That sounds like a dare, Mr. Wilder, and depending on the punishment, I might be tempted . . .*

She could almost hear his low, sexy growl as three dancing bubbles appeared on her screen while he formulated his carefully controlled response. *Take it however you like. You agreed to my rules, and one of them is security at all times.*

Even his text sounded so stern, and it definitely wasn't the inviting or seductive reply she'd been hoping for. Then again, he was dead set on being hands-off with her when she wanted his hands *on* her again. Everywhere.

She took a quick bite of her delicious omelet before delivering another wisecrack. *Security . . . as in you spying on me with all these cameras?* She looked up at the lens and stuck out her tongue playfully at him.

Just keeping an eye on my asset to make sure you keep out of trouble, brat.

She rolled her eyes up at him, realizing that she could have been talking directly to Maddux, rather than texting all this time. "Unfortunately, there is no trouble to be had here in your penthouse," she said in a wry tone as she set her phone face up on the counter and ate more of her breakfast. "But it's nice to know I'm not talking to myself."

Her phone buzzed and she glanced at his next incoming text. *Have a good day at work, Bella.*

"Maddux . . ." She beamed up at the camera and placed a hand on her chest. "That's *two* nice things you've done for me in one morning. Making me breakfast and wishing me a good day at work. I do believe there's a chance of reforming you after all."

Her phone vibrated on the counter. *Don't count on it, sweetheart. You have ten minutes to get your ass downstairs.*

She could easily imagine Maddux speaking those gruff words in that bossy, stern voice of his that made her panties damp and aroused her way too much. Which was crazy, since Gavin was plenty overbearing and all she'd ever felt toward his imperious attitude was irritation and displeasure.

Feeling naughty and wanting to stir a bit of Maddux's baser desires and give him something to rev his motor for the day, she playfully, obediently saluted him. "Yes, sir! I'm heading down right now."

Less than ten minutes later, she met up with Milo on the main level of the building, in the designated lobby area. The man was good-looking and about the same age as Maddux if she had to guess.

When they reached the black BMW he drove, he opened the passenger door for her and she slid inside, grateful that he wasn't making her sit in the backseat. On the drive to work, at least Milo was personable and talked to her, but any conversation about his employer, Maddux Wilder, was off-limits. Clearly, he was a loyal and trusted staff member for MadX-Tech who valued his job, and Arabella respected his fealty.

Mondays were always busy at the university library, which Arabella was grateful for because it kept her mind occupied and off of Maddux. Between research she had to get done, outstanding preservation projects that needed her attention, and a staff meeting that lasted most of the afternoon, the hours passed quickly.

Like most of her lunch breaks, instead of going out to a nearby restaurant with colleagues, she ordered something quick and easy from the campus dining area that could be delivered and eaten at her desk while she worked. While she was friendly with her co-workers, being the introvert that she was and always had been, those relationships were mostly superficial. A few of the women asked her about the fairy-tale ball she'd attended over the weekend—out of both curiosity and envy—and Arabella told them all what they were eager to hear... that it had been lavish, lively, and unforgettable.

It wasn't a lie. The Wilder Way charity ball had been all those things, even if the night had played out much differently than she ever could have imagined. Not that she shared her new living arrangements or her father's betrayal with any of them.

When five o'clock rolled around and she walked out of the library, Milo was waiting for her by the concrete steps, right where he'd been when she'd entered the building that morning.

"Catch any bad guys today during your watch?" she teased him.

An amused smile tugged at his lips. "No, ma'am. It was a very quiet and slow day."

"And boring, I'm sure." She fell into step beside her security guard, watching as he texted on his phone, certain she knew who he was corresponding with. "Tell Maddux that we're not coming back to the apartment right away," she said, which earned her a raised brow from Milo that made her grin. "Don't worry. I'm not going to try and make some big getaway. I just wanted to stop at that little Italian market we passed a block or so away from Maddux's building so I can pick up something to make for dinner."

"Okay," he said, and relayed the message.

Maddux must not have had an issue with her request, because Milo drove her directly to Moretti's Italian Grocery and Deli. As soon as she walked inside with her bodyguard at her side, an older man behind the deli counter greeted them with a huge, gregarious smile.

"Milo!" he called out merrily, clearly acquainted with Arabella's sidekick. "Nice to see you. And who is this beautiful lady you're with? A new girlfriend?"

Milo made a strangled, choking noise, his eyes wide. "Umm, no," he said, shaking his head quickly. "She . . . uh, belongs to Maddux."

Arabella burst out laughing at Milo's off-the-cuff description of her relationship with his employer. What was she, a pet poodle? Then again she couldn't refute that she *did* belong to Maddux. For now.

"I'm Luca Moretti," the older man introduced himself jovially, resting his arms on the high counter between them. "What can I do for this woman who belongs to Maddux Wilder?"

She felt her face warm at his teasing comment, but Luca clearly knew Maddux well, too. "Please, call me Arabella," she said, enjoying the other man's friendly nature.

"Ahhh . . ." Luca placed his hand over his heart, his dark brown eyes sparkling. "A beautiful name for such a beautiful, lovely woman."

"Husband, are you flirting with the pretty customers again?" a woman chastised as she came from a door that led to a back room. She looked to be in her late fifties, with dark hair, a gorgeous complexion, and a warm, friendly smile.

"Of course I am, my sweet Sofia. It keeps me young." Luca grabbed his wife's hand and drew her closer. "Come and meet Maddux's girlfriend, Arabella."

Sofia gasped. "This is like a rare unicorn sighting. We've never seen Maddux with a woman in here before, let alone met a girlfriend."

"I'm not his girlfriend," Arabella rushed to clarify, though her cheeks felt a few shades hotter at all the intimate references. "I'm just a friend." It was the most straightforward way to describe her odd relationship with Maddux.

Luca waggled a finger at her. "You can't fool us. That blush on your face says something much different."

"Let's let the girl be," Sofia said, her tone gentle. "We don't want to scare her away now that we've met her. What can we get for you, Arabella?"

"Well, let me see . . ." Grateful that the spotlight was now off of her, she gazed at all the items in the deli case . . . including fresh meats, sausages, sauces, homemade pasta, and side dishes. She'd planned to make something from scratch, but all the prepared entrees looked delicious, and considering how hungry she already was, just having to warm up an authentic Italian meal—no mess, no fuss—was suddenly very appealing.

"I'll take your rigatoni with the Italian meat sauce," she said. "Two servings, please."

"Ahhh, a romantic night in for two," Luca said in a fanciful tone as he started preparing her order.

She didn't want to burst his bubble and tell him that the table would most likely be set for one, not two, just as it had been last night. But at least Maddux would have something for dinner, when and if he decided to eat it.

Ten minutes later, Luca set a paper bag on the counter that was filled with the items she'd ordered, and Sofia joined her husband with a clear plastic to-go container of what looked like some kind of dessert that Arabella hadn't asked for.

Sofia smiled at her. "This is for the two of you to enjoy after dinner. Maddux loves my tiramisu and he hasn't stopped by in a while, and I always like to spoil him when I can."

"I'm sure he'll be happy to have your dessert," Arabella said as she withdrew her credit card from her wallet and handed it to Luca to pay for everything.

Luca held up a hand and shook his head.

"Oh, no, this is our treat," he insisted.

Sofia nodded her agreement beside her husband, her eyes soft and caring. "Maddux... he's done a lot for us. More than we can ever repay him for. Please, enjoy your dinner and dessert on us."

They were so sincere that Arabella didn't argue. "Okay, thank you. It was a pleasure meeting you both."

"You, as well," Luca said, settling his arm over his wife's shoulder. "Tell Maddux to not be a stranger, though he's clearly found better ways to pass his time than hanging out around here." The old man winked at her.

Arabella laughed, while Milo stepped forward and took her to-go bags for her. "I'll be sure to let him know."

From the Italian market, it didn't take long to reach Maddux's building, but it was enough time for Arabella to wonder about Sofia's intriguing comment, about Maddux doing so much for them, and more than they could ever repay. The couple clearly adored Maddux and thought highly of him, which meant her brusque and boorish beast had a charitable side to him. As much as he'd like her to believe he wasn't a nice guy, she'd seen too many glimpses to the contrary.

Right now, Maddux Wilder was an angry man lashing out, but at the core of who he was, Luca and Sofia had just revealed to her that there was a man who was kind, caring, and generous. He'd somehow helped the couple, and they were grateful for whatever he'd done for them.

Arabella wanted to know that compassionate man, and even more foolishly, she wanted to be the woman who took away his pain and hatred and replaced it with tenderness and affection.

An impossible wish, considering her father was his mortal enemy and she was merely the pawn between them.

CHAPTER FIFTEEN

ARABELLA WALKED INTO the lobby of the building with Milo accompanying her, surprised to see Maddux talking to two uniformed police officers. She was even more shocked to find Gavin there, as well, standing stiffly beside one of the cops. As soon as she entered, her heels clicking on the smooth stone floor, everyone turned and looked at her... the officers with concern, Gavin with an arrogant, possessive stare, and as for Maddux, she couldn't read his neutral expression at all, though the clench of his jaw gave her a hint of his irritation.

Dismissing Gavin altogether, she walked right past him and stopped next to Maddux instead—not thinking twice about where her loyalty automatically gravitated to. "Is everything okay?" The fact that Gavin was there with law enforcement made her distinctly uncomfortable.

Before Maddux could say anything, Gavin jumped in. "Jesus, Arabella! I've been worried sick about you. You haven't returned my calls or answered my texts. I'm here to get you out of this messed-up situation!"

He stepped toward her, and it was a good thing that one of the police officers put his hand out to hold Gavin back, because Maddux's entire body tensed, and his hands curled into fists at his sides. No doubt, he wasn't going to let Gavin touch her, and that protective demeanor gave her a dizzying rush of pleasure.

With a calm that belied the undercurrent of rage churning through him for his adversary, Maddux met her gaze, his voice composed. "The police are here for a welfare check."

"Welfare check?" she echoed, dumbfounded.

One of the cops nodded toward Gavin. "Mr. Scott here claims that you're being held against your will by Maddux Wilder."

"I'm fine," she said, looking both of the officers in the eyes so they could see she wasn't hiding anything.

"You don't have to lie, Arabella," Gavin said, his tone enraged. "Tell them the truth, that he's holding you captive."

She laughed at his insistence as she came to the realization that if she had to choose between leaving with Gavin or staying with Maddux, it was a surprisingly easy decision. And remaining with Maddux wasn't about protecting her father anymore . . . it was about the possibility of exploring her forbidden desires with a man who'd unearthed them and discovering the woman she was meant to be. However, getting Maddux on board with that idea was much more difficult than she would have thought considering the hands-off approach he'd suddenly erected between them, but she wasn't done trying to seduce him into changing his mind.

"I don't know what you're talking about," she said, addressing Gavin directly. "I just spent the day at work and stopped at a market down the street. I'm free to come and go as I please." Okay, not one hundred percent the truth. She could leave as long as she had a security guard with her, but she honestly didn't feel restricted at all.

"He's already brainwashed you," Gavin hissed, then glared at Milo, who was standing casually off to the side. "And what about this guy? Who is he?"

"That's Milo. My driver." She shrugged. "He took me to work and picked me up."

Gavin's complexion reddened, and it was all he could do to keep his temper in check.

"Well, that's about all we can do here," one of the officers said, and glanced at Arabella. "You don't appear to be in distress and you're in good health, and there isn't anything suspicious or illegal going on that we can see, so we'll be on our way."

The other cop gave Maddux a polite nod. "Thank you for your time, Mr. Wilder. We apologize for bothering you."

They turned to leave, forcing Gavin to follow them out, but not before he shot a dark, violent look at Maddux. The other man was unmistakably pissed off that his efforts had been thwarted.

"Everything okay here?" Milo asked Maddux, a thread of concern in his voice as he handed Arabella the grocery bag he'd been holding. "Or do you need me to stay with Arabella?"

Maddux shook his head. "She'll be secure up in the penthouse. She'll see you the same time tomorrow morning."

Milo nodded. "I'll be here. You two have a good evening."

Maddux pressed his hand against her lower back and escorted her toward the elevator. Once they were enclosed inside, he pressed the two button, which was where the MadX-Tech offices were located, and then the M button. It appeared she was heading up to his apartment alone. She was disappointed but not surprised.

"Well, that was interesting," she said, referring to the welfare check.

"Indeed." Maddux pushed his hands into the pockets of his dress pants and studied Arabella curiously. "You had the perfect opportunity to tell those officers I was holding you hostage and against your will, but you didn't."

"You're not holding me hostage, Maddux," she said with a smile as the elevator doors opened on the MadX-Tech floor. "Maybe I'm starting to *want* to be here, despite your vendetta against my father."

His gaze held hers as he stared at her for a long moment, conflicting emotions chasing across his gorgeous expression before he shuttered them all, but not before she saw his desire... and the want and need that reflected her own. That intense look stole her breath and her heart beat wildly in her chest at the possibility of him giving in to that deep, intimate longing that was getting stronger and stronger between them.

But just as the doors started to close, he slipped out, crushing any hope she might have had that her decision to stay of her own free will changed his mind about getting closer to her. She'd just have to keep trying. She was nothing if not persistent.

HE WAS OBSESSED with Arabella. There was no other explanation for the way she invaded his thoughts all day long while he was working or the compelling urge he had to keep an eye on her in his penthouse even when he wasn't there. He even liked how easily she'd already made herself at home, and especially enjoyed the gregarious way she talked to him via the security cameras. It was insane, but he'd smiled more times in the short period since she'd moved in than he had in the past year because of her affable personality.

Not wanting to miss watching Arabella in action, as soon as he arrived back in his main office, he sat at his desk and turned on the monitor displaying the various angles of his apartment. Christ, he was becoming a fucking creeper, but he couldn't deny that he was beginning to crave this woman in ways that had him tied up in knots inside. He did his best to avoid spending time alone with her, yet every chance he had, Maddux had his eyes on her. The contradictory actions weren't lost on him.

He found her in the kitchen, unloading whatever she'd purchased at Moretti's onto the counter. She set two round aluminum tins on the stove, turned on the oven, then glanced up at the camera. He sat up straighter in his chair, anticipating the conversation to come.

"I bought two servings of rigatoni with meat sauce so you wouldn't have to worry about dinner," she said, talking to him as if he was right in front of her. "And Sofia insisted on packaging up some of her tiramisu for you, as well, which she said was your favorite."

At the mention of those two items, his stomach growled hungrily. He'd had a busy day with meetings and calls and hadn't had time to eat lunch, and quite frankly, he was starved.

"I'm going to put your rigatoni in the oven to heat it with mine, in hopes that I can convince you to join me for dinner tonight. I'd really love the company." She exhaled a deep breath, a hint of vulnerability softening her features. "I just . . . really don't want to spend another evening alone."

The fact that she wore her emotions so completely on her sleeve thawed a little more of Maddux's resolve to keep the walls between them nice and high and insurmountable. She turned back to the stove and slid the heatable containers into the oven to warm the food inside, then without saying another word or looking at the camera again, she left the kitchen.

He didn't like the feeling of being . . . ignored. How fucking ironic was that? He followed her trek through the living room, where she kicked off her heels, then padded in her bare feet out the French doors leading to the terrace. Hands braced on the railing, she looked out over the view, and he couldn't get her words out of his head. *I don't want to spend another evening alone.*

He scrubbed a hand along the light beard growth on his jawline, feeling those contained and guarded parts of his psyche slowly caving to the soft, imploring way she'd asked him to join her. He knew what it felt like to be alone, and though he'd spent the past fourteen years living that way by choice, for once he just wanted to enjoy a woman's company beyond something sexual. Not just any woman, he amended, but Arabella, specifically.

He justified that it was just a meal, and he had enough self-control to eat dinner with a woman without crossing any physical lines. Once dinner was over, he could retreat to his penthouse office until she was asleep for the evening, then he'd join her, because he didn't relish the thought of spending another night tossing and turning on the hard, uncomfortable couch in his apartment office as he had the evening before.

Decision made, he stood up and removed his work tie and hung it on a hook behind the office door, where his suit jacket was, then unfastened the first five buttons down his shirt and rolled the sleeves up to his forearms so he was more comfortable and casual. He took the elevator to his apartment, then made his way out to the terrace, where Arabella was still standing, a slight, cool spring breeze feathering through her unbound hair.

As soon as she heard his footsteps, she turned around, surprise and delight widening her big blue eyes at the sight of him, and damn if her unconcealed joy didn't make him want to smile. It took effort not to be a total sap and grin.

"You came!" she said on a rush of breath, her excitement palpable as she clasped her hands in front of her.

He pushed his fists into the front pockets of his slacks. "It was the tiramisu that lured me," he teased, surprising himself with the humorous tone of his voice.

She stepped toward him and raised a brow, her expression equally playful. "Was that *all* that lured you?"

Her. Always her. God, what was happening to him? She was like a beacon of light to his darkness, drawing him closer and closer.

"And I'm hungry," he admitted, unwilling to confess how much being in her company had factored into his decision.

"Okay, I'll take it," she said happily. "Dinner should be just about warmed up, so I'll go and plate it. It's such a lovely night out. How about we eat out here on the terrace?" she suggested, indicating the outdoor table he rarely used.

"Sounds good. While you're getting dinner, I'll grab us a bottle of wine to go with the meal."

"Perfect!" Grinning enthusiastically, she passed him on her way to the kitchen, a visible bounce to her step.

Maddux made a quick trip to his wine cellar, selecting a mellow Pinot Noir that would pair nicely with a tomato-based red sauce. He grabbed two wineglasses and met Arabella back out on the terrace just as she was setting two plates of steaming rigatoni on the table, along with napkins and silverware. They sat across from one another, he poured them each a good portion of the Pinot Noir, and they started eating the delicious meal. The whole situation almost felt domestic . . . and more comfortable than he would have expected.

A few bites in, she dabbed her napkin across her mouth and glanced across the table at him. "I really enjoyed meeting Luca and Sofia," she said of the Morettis. "They were warm and kind, and they think very highly of you."

"Surprised?" he asked wryly, taking a drink of his wine.

"No. Not at all," she said with a shake of her head. "For sure, you're a mix of contradictions. I mean, you've kind of given me whiplash over the last few days with your shifting moods, but despite how surly you can be, I'm also starting to see how much you care about certain people around you. Your siblings. Milo. And the Morettis, for starters. I understand that I'm the exception and your brusque attitude toward me stems from whatever is between you and my father, but despite all your attempts to make me believe you're this mercenary beast, I don't believe that's who you truly are deep inside."

Whoa. Maddux processed her astute comment as he ate a bite of his dinner. Her insight shouldn't have surprised him considering she was an idealist who tended to see the good in people—Gavin withstanding, because the guy was a royal dick—but Maddux didn't want Arabella prying into his character and unearthing the part of him he reserved for the people he cared about or loved, which was an incredibly small circle . . . so why was he tempted to reveal more of the man he was beneath all the pain and anger that had driven him for fourteen long years when no other woman had ever prompted such an urge?

"But don't worry," she went on affably after taking a drink of wine, unaware of his internal struggle to constantly keep his emotional walls up around her. "I promise not to tell anyone that you're a really nice guy and ruin your boorish reputation."

"I appreciate that," he said, keeping a straight face.

She pushed a few of the noodles around on her dish before glancing across the table at him, her expression suddenly thoughtful. "Can I ask you something?"

No. That's what he should have said and shut down whatever serious question was coming his way, but his mouth and brain didn't cooperate. "Yes."

"Luca and Sofia said that they owed you . . . that you've done a lot for them and more than they could ever repay." Her voice was soft and curious. "What did you do to help them?"

Arabella didn't realize it, but her question was a loaded, explosive one, and the honest answer would undoubtedly send her reeling in shock. Six years ago, when Maddux had first started purchasing real estate in the area, along with rebuilding the low-income areas and helping to restore small fledgling businesses that were about to go under, Maddux had learned that Theodore and Gavin had quietly claimed the neighborhood as their own little financial playground.

Every month, they demanded lofty payments from the stores and markets with sole proprietorships in exchange for "protection" that the businesses didn't need. But *not* making those payments resulted in threats, accidents, and casualties . . . exactly what had happened to

Maddux's own parents.

He'd been fucking livid when he'd discovered the underhanded scheme and the fact that Theodore and Gavin were trolling a neighborhood that was now Maddux's turf. When he'd learned that Luca and Sofia had been on the verge of bankruptcy and being destitute as a result of being bilked for every bit of their monthly profits, Maddux had sent an explicit warning to Theodore and Gavin... step foot anywhere near his properties again and Maddux would break every fucking bone in their bodies and bury them in a place where only maggots would ever find them.

It had been his first power play toward the two pricks who'd destroyed Maddux's family, and even though it had taken him six more years to be in the position to finally take Theodore completely under with the right leverage, the Morettis, along with the other businesses in the neighborhood, had been grateful for *Maddux's* protection, which hadn't cost them a thing.

Arabella was watching him expectantly, still waiting for some kind of answer from him. Maddux downed the rest of his wine and refilled his glass, suddenly needing something much stronger to navigate his way through this emotional minefield with Arabella, and himself... because as much as he knew he ought to tell her the truth about her father's corrupt ways, which would effectively put a much-needed wedge between himself and Arabella, something held him back.

Fuck... he just couldn't bring himself to devastate her so callously. It was Theodore who'd destroyed so many lives, and Arabella, who was completely innocent to her father's dirty dealings, shouldn't have to pay the price for his offenses. Yet Maddux was aware that she'd discover the truth about everything eventually... just not tonight.

After another long swallow of wine that nearly depleted the alcohol in his glass, he met her gaze. "I helped Luca and Sofia when they were in a tough financial situation."

It wasn't a lie. Even after Theodore had received Maddux's message and stopped demanding money from the small businesses in the area, it had taken all those owners a long time to recover from the monetary strain Theodore had put upon them for years. And in an effort to save those businesses, Maddux had offered as much financial assistance as he could to keep those stores open and afloat... without asking for any compensation in return.

Arabella set her fork down on her empty plate, gazing at him with respect and an awe he didn't want or deserve. "See... more proof that you're a good guy, Maddux Wilder."

She stood and picked up both of their plates. "And now, tiramisu for dessert," she announced. "I'll be back in a few minutes."

He watched her head back into the kitchen

and could hear her washing their dirty dishes and putting any leftovers away. And even though he knew she was going to return with dessert, he realized that he couldn't, and shouldn't, just sit here and enjoy her company while pretending that this was a normal, pleasurable night in with Arabella. It wasn't his life, and it wasn't going to last.

Yet despite every denial he wanted to cling to, he couldn't ignore the truth... that he was already getting attached to this sweet, affectionate woman who saw beneath his terse façade and called him on his bullshit. He was starting to care, and that was a very dangerous thing in a situation where letting his emotions get involved would fuck up everything he'd planned for the past fourteen long years.

Refusing to think about how disappointed Arabella was going to be, he stood up and quietly made his way back to his office, making sure she didn't see him on the way through the living room. He didn't want to have to explain why he was holing himself up yet again, especially after a nice dinner together. This way was easier. Simpler. She'd walk out to the veranda in a few minutes, realize he was gone, and accept it as his normal MO.

He was becoming a regular Houdini as far as she was concerned.

CHAPTER SIXTEEN

ARABELLA HAD BEEN eager to sample Sofia's tiramisu, and had been even more excited to spend extra time with Maddux, instead of alone. But the joke was on her, because as soon as she stepped out on the terrace and found him gone, she knew exactly where he'd disappeared to, and that she wouldn't see him for the rest of the evening.

Not wanting to eat dessert alone, she exhaled a defeated sigh and took the two plates back to the kitchen. After placing both slices of tiramisu into a sealed container, she put them into the refrigerator. She didn't so much as glance at the cameras directed her way, closing Maddux off the same way he'd just shut her out. Yes, he could see her and watch her, but she wasn't going to give him the satisfaction of acknowledging him in any way. As stupid as she knew it was—because Maddux had never claimed to be Mr. Warm and Fuzzy—after their nice dinner together, his dismissive attitude hurt.

So instead, she spent the next few hours in his lavish bathroom with the door locked, ensuring her privacy. She filled the tub, adding a few of the vanilla lavender bath oil beads she'd found in the toiletries Maddux's guys had brought from her place. As the water rose toward the brim and fragrant steam filled the enclosed area, she stripped out of her work clothes, pinned up her hair, then sank into the warm bath.

She stayed in there for nearly two hours thanks to the self-heating tub and finished the book she was reading. Completely relaxed and ready to go to bed, she finally got out of the bath, dried off, and changed into her favorite dark blue silk shift she liked to sleep in. Back in Maddux's room, she once again ignored the cameras as she unpinned her hair and cleaned up her things. Walking to what she now thought of as her side of the mattress, she switched on the lamp and stared in confusion at the stack of older-looking books on the nightstand that she hadn't put there.

Her breath caught in her chest when she realized what they were. Not just any ordinary set of books, they were the collection of first edition Jane Austen novels she'd bid on at the Wilder Way charity event on Saturday. The same set that someone else had won at the steep price that had gone well over one hundred grand.

She ran her fingers over the surface of the top book, her heart pounding with pleasure and delight. There was no doubt in her mind that it had been Maddux who'd left the books there for her. Maddux who'd paid an astronomical amount for the rare editions she'd coveted for herself. He must have seen her that night, had watched her place a bid, and when it had reached over six figures, he'd offered the last amount to seal the deal. For her. *But why?*

She swallowed back the emotional knot gathering in her throat. He didn't have to buy the first editions, and he certainly didn't have to offer them to her as a gift under any circumstances. But he had, and she wanted so badly to believe that his actions spoke to something deeper between them, because most people didn't give someone they disliked such a special, indulgent gift that clearly meant so much to them—as these books meant to her.

It took everything in her to resist the urge to turn around and face the security camera in the room, to thank Maddux and let him see the joy on her face and tell him how much she loved and appreciated the rare books. That the kind, thoughtful gesture he'd made had her overflowing with warmth and gratitude and affection for him.

But talking to an inanimate object was too impersonal, and she wanted, and craved, that intimate, face-to-face interaction with Maddux. Making a split-second decision, she headed toward the other side of his penthouse, certain he was tracking her movement every step of the way via his cameras. When she reached his office, she walked in without knocking on the closed door.

Judging by the casual way he was leaning back

in his leather chair and the lack of surprise on his face, he'd been expecting her. He held an almost empty glass of dark liquid she assumed was hard liquor, and his expression was unreadable as she walked toward him, though his eyes did take note of the thigh-length silk shift she was wearing, and her nipples tightened against the cool fabric as a sensual awareness flowed through her veins.

She lifted her chin a few stubborn inches. "I know I'm probably racking up a punishment for barging in here, but I know you saw me coming, and I didn't want you to tell me to leave you alone without having the chance to walk into your office so I could talk to you, in person, face-to-face."

"Okay," he said simply as he swirled the last bit of alcohol in his glass, shocking her with his agreeable demeanor when she'd been anticipating a more contentious response.

She rounded his desk so she was standing next to his chair, so close she could reach out and touch him if she wanted. But she didn't. "Maddux . . . you can't just leave a gift like that for me without saying a word." Her words were soft and threaded with emotion.

His gaze held hers, his still carefully shuttered. "I believe I did."

"Why would you do it, Maddux?" she asked, needing to hear his answer, his reasons. "Why would you bid on those books, pay a small fortune for them, then give them to me, of all people?"

He tossed back the rest of the amber liquid, set the glass on the desk, then rocked back in his chair, a slight frown forming between his brows. "Honestly?"

"Yes." She wanted, needed, the truth.

"I bought them out of spite, because I saw that you wanted them and I didn't want you to have them," he said, his voice rough as gravel as he admitted his intentions. "Didn't matter the cost, because it went to charity. It wasn't about the amount of money . . . that night, it was about taking something you wanted because it gave me a twisted sense of pleasure considering everything going on with your father."

There was no vindictiveness in his tone, just a regret that spoke volumes. His actions might have originally been based on anger and disdain, but that wasn't the case now or he wouldn't have left the books on her nightstand. "So why did you give them to me?"

He paused a moment, as if he was hesitant about revealing his reasons, but finally gave her the insight she longed for. "Because now, I want you to have the books. Despite how much I hate your father . . . I don't hate you, and those books are meant to be yours because I know you'll treasure them."

"I will," she whispered, giving him a tremulous smile. "Thank you so much."

A slight, bittersweet smile touched the corner

of his lips. "You're welcome, Bella."

God . . . her heart couldn't contain all the varying emotions she was suddenly feeling for this paradoxical man. And how much he'd come to mean to her in such a short time. There was so much goodness beneath all his pain, and Arabella wanted him more than she'd ever needed anything else in her entire life. Except for all his promises to fuck her, to do dirty, wicked things to her that her body longed for, he'd backed off when that was the last thing she wanted, and she decided to call him out on the way he'd been deliberately skirting that physical contact with her.

"Why are you avoiding me?" she asked.

"I've been busy," he replied.

That was a crock of polite, easy bullshit to avoid the real reason he was keeping distance between them. This time, she looked him directly in the eyes and didn't mince her words. "Let me rephrase that. Why won't you fuck me, when that was part of our agreement?"

Her bold, direct question definitely got his attention, though she hadn't anticipated the annoyance that etched his features. "Because you're not ready for me to fuck you, and you still have a lot to learn," he said, brusque and blunt.

She stepped in front of him, between his spread legs, and saw his pupils darken. "Then teach me *everything*."

He groaned deep in his throat. "Bella, as much as I want you, I have no right to take your virginity. It doesn't fucking belong to me."

He sounded angry, and she almost laughed at the thought that somewhere along the way her assertive beast had grown a conscience, when she was desperate for the dominant man who'd held her down in the bathtub the other day and demanded her body submit to his pleasure. Just the thought of that provocative memory made her sex pulse with need.

"I'm going to be very clear about this," she said, taking a direct and candid approach as she reached out and caressed the tips of her fingers along the soft, short growth of beard on his jaw, aching to feel that facial hair abrading the tender, sensitive skin of her inner thighs. "I'm not a prim, timid, innocent maiden from the eighteenth century. I'm a twenty-five-year-old grown *woman* who knows her own mind. You're not *taking* my virginity like some antiquated caveman. I'm giving it to you, openly and deliberately, without any doubts or reservations, because it's what *I* want with *you*."

Beneath her fingertips, she felt his jaw clench. "I don't fucking deserve it," he said on a low, agitated growl. "You should save it for a man who does."

"Shouldn't I get to decide who deserves to be the first man to fuck me?" She swallowed hard, realizing she didn't want Maddux to just be her first. She wanted him to be the one and only man to have that privilege, which was a ridiculous thought considering her time with him was only temporary, and there was no way he'd ever want anything more than just a hookup with his enemy's daughter.

"I want that man to be you, Maddux," she reiterated, and deciding to up the stakes, she pushed the thin straps of her nightgown off her shoulders, then lowered her arms and let the silky fabric fall to the floor at her feet, leaving her standing in front of him in just a pair of lacy panties. "It's my body, my choice, my pleasure . . . and I choose you."

His breathing deepened as his gaze raked over her bare breasts, his growing erection straining against the front of his slacks. His hands curled into fists on the arms of the chair, as if he was struggling not to touch everything she was offering. "The way I want to fuck you isn't sweet or gentle or romantic."

His words rang out like a warning, but it was a foreshadowing that was unnecessary because Arabella was already well aware that Maddux enjoyed exerting authority over her physical responses . . . and her body *loved* yielding to his commands.

"I know," she said, and brazenly straddled his lap on the chair, tucking her knees on either side of his hips while her fingers finished unfastening the rest of the buttons on his shirt so she could touch his bare skin. "You have to know, based on the things we've already done, that sweet, gentle, and romantic isn't what I want, either."

His eyes blazed with frustration and fire as they stared into hers, but he didn't touch her despite the fact that she was sitting on his thighs half-naked, her hair tumbling around her shoulders and curling right above the swells of her breasts. His entire body was tense, his restraint admirable, but she didn't want his chivalrous gesture about saving her virginity, and she was determined to fracture his admirable control. The thought of him snapping and going all alpha male on her caused Arabella to shiver in anticipation.

"I have waited a very long time to come across a man who makes me feel the way you do," she went on, parting the sides of his shirt to give her a better view of his wide shoulders, his broad chest, and those tight abs she wanted to lick. "A man who is *real*, and not just a figment of my dirty fantasies when I need to get off when I'm alone in my bed at night or a dominant, fictional hero I read about in one of my books."

Upping her game, she placed her hands over her breasts, fondling them as he watched. "You touch me, and I burn and ache." She pulled at her nipples, having learned from Maddux that she liked that edge of pain that arrowed its way down to her core. "You give me that dark, lust-filled look, the exact one you're giving me right now, and I get hot and restless and wetter than I thought was even possible."

A low, rumbling noise rose from his chest, his

expression dangerously threatening. "*You need to fucking stop*," he said though his clenched teeth.

"No, *you* need to give me what I want," she said, smiling at him oh so sweetly, contradicting the naughty way she rolled her hips and rubbed her sex along the length of his rigid shaft. Despite the barrier of his pants and her underwear, the pressure and friction had him hissing out a harsh stream of breath.

She flattened her hands on his pecs and skimmed her thumbs over his hard nipples, then leaned in closer, until her lips touched the side of his neck without the scars, and moved up toward his ear. "You make me feel wanted and desired like no one ever has before," she whispered, sharing her deepest secrets with him. "My body responds to your demands in ways that I always thought were forbidden or wrong, but how can something that feels so damn good be anything but perfectly right?"

"Arabella, *stop*." He barked out the order, using her full name in a firm tone that did nothing to dissuade her.

"I want to experience this, and you, for as long as it lasts," she went on, placing a warm kiss at his throat before lifting her head and looking into amber eyes that were broiling with a raw lust and need she wanted to see crack and spill over for her.

She settled her hands on either side of his face, feeling emotionally exposed and vulnerable as she laid a part of her heart bare and gave him all she had left. "The night you took me in exchange for my father, you demanded my total surrender, Maddux. I gave it to you. Take it. *Please*. It's yours. *I'm* yours."

The change in him happened so fast, Arabella was unprepared for the sudden, tumultuous transformation... from a determined man keeping his desires on lock-down to the sudden power that shifted through his big, strapping body as he took charge. It was startling and exhilarating. It was exactly what she'd asked for, yet she couldn't contain her gasp as he plowed all ten of his fingers through her hair, gripped the strands in his fists, and jerked her mouth up to his.

Her hands landed on his chest for support, and like a violent storm unleashed, his firm lips brutally pushed hers apart, providing the entrance he wanted for the deep, invading thrust of his tongue. A possessive growl erupted from his throat as his mouth ravaged hers, the kiss rough, ruthless, and nothing short of uncivilized.

Arabella had the fleeting thought that she'd pushed him to this... and she was glad she had because instead of shock or fear, his pure dominance filled her with a thrilling, provocative power of her own and spiked her desire to intoxicating, addicting levels where she wanted, and needed, *more*.

When he finally released her mouth, he was breathing hard as he stared down into her eyes.

"Want to know how dark and dirty I can get, Bella?" he rasped, and all she could manage was a whimper and an eager nod that resulted in an approving, wicked smile appearing on his lips. "Yeah, you want it so fucking dirty, don't you, sweet girl?"

His hands untangled from her hair and gripped her hips. He yanked her forward, fitting the thick length of his erection against the front panel of her already soaked panties, nudging hard against her drenched flesh and needy clit. The ache in her sex built, and she shamelessly rubbed up against his dick like a cat in heat.

"Yeah, grind your pussy all over my cock," he murmured, his heavy-lidded gaze on her face as he grabbed her ass in his hands and rolled her hips tighter and harder against his. "Give me a filthy lap dance and make yourself come just like this. I'm going to need you nice and soft and slick in order to bury myself as deep as I need to go in your tight pussy. That's what you want, right?"

Her head nodded jerkily, and she panted and squirmed eagerly against him. "Yes, please."

He gave her a lascivious smile as he smacked her ass with the flat of his palm, making her gasp at the delicious burn spreading across her backside and down between her thighs. "Then get to work, sweetheart, and give yourself that orgasm."

He twisted his fingers into her hair again, this time to pull her head back and force her to arch her spine, which offered up her breasts to his mouth. He captured a nipple, and the hot, suctioning pull on that tender nub of flesh, followed by the swirl of his tongue, and finishing with the wicked scrape of his teeth drove her wild. With every bite, with every firm lick, her nipples swelled until they were so tender and sensitive it was like he had a direct line to teasing her clit.

"Fuck my dick harder," he ordered, nipping at the curve of her neck, his breathing hot and damp on her skin. "I want you so fucking wet I get lost deep inside of your pussy."

Inarticulate sounds rose up from her throat. His dirty words pushed her to the verge of detonating, and she instinctively rocked against the rigid column of his shaft, mindlessly thrusting and gyrating her hips, her entire being expanding with white-hot passion. The need for release made her delirious, overwhelming her with a sizzling rush of pleasure so intense she could only gasp and claw at his shoulders while her body pulsed, shuddered, and she finally collapsed against his chest.

He gently stroked a hand up and down her back as she recovered, his mouth near her ear. "When I stand up, put your arms around my neck and wrap your legs around my waist."

"Where are you taking me?" she asked, forcing herself to lift her head and look into his eyes, even though she felt so lethargic after that gargantuan orgasm. "We're not finished, are we?"

He must have heard the touch of panic in her voice, the fear that he was going to leave her unfulfilled once again, and shook his head. "No, sweet girl, we're not finished," he murmured huskily. "That was just the first phase of corrupting you."

She secured her arms around his neck as he'd instructed, her fingers absently threading through his long, unruly hair. Though his own body was still tense from *his* lack of release, his earlier edgy disposition was gone, leaving behind a man who clearly was no longer struggling between resisting her and wanting her. Nor was he going to deny them what they both desired.

She raised a curious brow. "What is the second phase?"

His eyes darkened, and a sinfully seductive smile curved his lips. "Phase two is tying you to my bed and licking and eating and sucking your clit until you scream my name as you come again, and then driving my cock as deep as I can inside your pussy so I can feel you come all over my dick."

She bit her bottom lip, completely on board with that plan. "Then what are you waiting for? I would like the complete corruption package, please."

Her teasing comment drew a warm chuckle from him that she loved hearing. "Duly noted, Bella," he said, standing up, holding her effortlessly in his arms as he started toward his bedroom and a night of delightful impropriety and decadent pleasures.

CHAPTER SEVENTEEN

Maddux carried Arabella through his penthouse, her arms anchored around his neck, her soft, slender legs clinging to his waist, and his big hands cupping her small, firm ass to hold her up. With their faces in such close proximity and her eyes soft with desire for him, she settled her seductive mouth against his, kissing him more slowly and sweetly than he'd ever been kissed before.

She was a lightweight and there wasn't much furniture in his penthouse to dodge, so making his way to the other side of the apartment, even with her distracting him, wasn't difficult. With her hands tugging at his hair, she slid her tongue teasingly along his lower lip, playfully tugged on that bit of flesh with her teeth, and he opened up to her exploration, letting her enjoy her brief upper hand, because once they were in his bedroom, he was going to be one hundred percent in charge.

Once they arrived, he let her slide down his hard, excruciatingly aroused body until her feet touched the floor. "Get up on the bed," he ordered.

She climbed up onto the mattress while he disappeared into his closet, where he stripped off the rest of his clothes except for his boxer briefs. Then he withdrew a silk tie from one of his drawers and walked back into the bedroom, pleased to see her reclining on the comforter.

"Put your hands above your head and grip the slats in the headboard," he said, coming closer.

She blinked at him, looking surprised by the request, and he smirked as he ran the strip of silk through his hands. "Did you think I was kidding when I said I was going to tie you to my bed?"

When he was standing by the side of the mattress, her gaze traveled down his bare chest, then lower, to the thick erection that would soon know what it was like to be cushioned in the snug warmth of her body.

She licked her lips and raised her eyes back to his. "I . . . umm . . . guess I wasn't sure."

"Be *very* sure, Bella, because I don't say things for the shock value of it. You *will* be bound to my bed, and I *am* going to devour all that sweetness between your pretty thighs until you come on my tongue and I'm satisfied you're lubricated enough to take all of me."

Her skin flushed at his explicit words, her nipples tightening into ripe berries crowning her pert breasts, but she didn't hesitate to raise her arms above her head and curl her fingers around the sturdy wooden bars. Her acquiescence drove his lust for her ten times higher.

"Good girl," he murmured, leaning over to secure her wrists and make sure the rest of the material held her arms in place. Then he opened the nightstand and retrieved a condom.

"Maddux . . ." Her voice was as vulnerable as her gaze as she captured his attention. "What if I don't want anything between us?"

He shook his head, even as his dick twitched at the thought of being inside her completely bare. "I'm not going to risk you getting pregnant." He'd come to terms with being the man to take her virginity, because it's what *she* wanted, but protecting her, in every way, was his first priority.

"I'm on the pill . . . to regulate my periods . . . have been for years." She shifted nervously on the bed, clearly not used to having these kinds of conversations. "So, if *you're* good, this is what I want for my first time. Just you. All of you. Please."

Jesus, this woman shredded him, and something near the vicinity of his heart loosened with a softer, deeply affectionate emotion. "I'm clean," he assured her. As a part of his personal life insurance, he underwent regular testing, and he hadn't been with a woman since his last *all clear* report.

While she watched, he slid his thumbs into the waistband of his underwear and pushed it down and off. She'd seen him naked before in the bathroom, but her gaze ate him up, and her chest rose and fell with deeper breaths... and they hadn't even started yet.

He rounded to the foot of the bed, moved on top of the mattress, then quickly and easily removed her panties. He tossed them onto the floor, then looked up at her, amused at the prim way she pressed her thighs together. As much as he intended to strip away any inhibition she might have left in her tonight, her suddenly modest demeanor fed into his more dominant side that wanted to conquer and command and get off on watching her submit to his directions.

"Spread your legs, Bella," he said, his voice direct. "Nice and wide so I can fit my shoulders in between."

Her knees parted, but only slight enough to give him a tiny peek of the shadowed treasure in between. For her disobedience, he slid his hand up her leg and pinched the tender flesh of her inner thigh. Her hands reflexively jerked on the bonds around her wrists as a startled, pained squeak erupted from her mouth. Her eyes were as round as saucers, but she didn't look upset or afraid. No, the excitement that flickered in her eyes assured him she was just fine.

"That was to get your attention. When I tell you to do something, I expect you to obey the *first* time I ask," he said, even as he feathered his thumb across the skin he'd tweaked, soothing away any lingering sting.

"This is what you asked for," he reminded

her, pinning her with a severe look. "This is what you *begged* me for. Now look at the width of my shoulders and give me the room I need to make myself comfortable when I'm lying between your thighs."

She exhaled on a ragged breath that made her stomach quiver and separated her feet *far* apart this time, giving him a hot, direct view of her pretty pink pussy, full lips, plump clit, and all that sweet cream waiting for him to lap up. He didn't waste any time settling right there at the gates of heaven. Ignoring the way his heavy, pulsing cock dug into the mattress, he arranged each of her legs over his shoulders and opened his mouth over her sex.

She immediately moaned, and her thighs trembled as he gave her a slow, thorough lick that ended with the tip of his tongue flicking against her clit. Her hips bucked, and he pushed one long finger into her tight sheath, then two. She sucked in a startled breath, her body tensing at the invasion and clamping down on those two digits, making his head spin at the thought of how fucking incredible she was going to feel surrounding his sizable dick.

He groaned and instinctively ground his erection into the mattress, trying to stave off the need to rut and focusing everything on Arabella's pleasure. She was so slick and warm, and he stretched her, readying her body to take the full length of him while devouring her pussy with his mouth and the slip-slide of his tongue until he eventually felt her inner muscles start to give way to the fingers thrusting as deep as they could go.

Her soft, keening cry reached his ears, and her hips started moving of their own accord, trying to chase the orgasm he was slowly, gradually building with the glide of his thumb over her clit and every pass of his tongue. He wanted it to be fucking *huge*. As her arousal grew, as she gave herself over to his sensual torment, more of her juices slicked his fingers, which was exactly what he needed to ease the way for his cock when the time came . . . which was going to be soon.

"Maddux," she whimpered desperately, her arms pulling at the tie securing her hands to the headboard while her lower body writhed against his mouth and the slow, deep pump of his fingers stroking in and out of her.

"Please, please, please," she begged deliriously.

He gave her body what it was so greedy for. Her breathing shallowed as he swirled and sucked the swollen nub of her clitoris. When he deliberately rubbed the pad of his fingers against that soft, sensitive patch of skin inside her vaginal walls, her entire body stiffened as her orgasm crashed through her, and she screamed until her voice was hoarse and she finally sank back down to the mattress in a boneless heap.

Maddux sat up between her spread thighs, the ache in his cock and balls beyond anything he could ever remember experiencing. All he knew was that he needed to be inside of Arabella, and it had nothing to do with taking her virginity, but fusing his body intimately to hers so that he could make her *his*.

He glanced up at her face, her expression replete and her blue eyes dark and soft and sultry, matching the sensual smile on her lips.

"I'm ready, Maddux," she whispered oh so sweetly, her gorgeous body his for the pilfering.

"Are you sure?" he asked, his voice a rasp of sound, but he had to know she hadn't changed her mind. That she still wanted this. Wanted him.

She gave him a mock frown, that playfulness he loved about her etching her features. "Don't make me ask twice."

He laughed... fucking *laughed* during sex, with Arabella still tied up and his cock dripping with pre-come. He wanted the pleasure she was about to give him. He wanted the orgasm and release. But as he settled his body over the top of hers and braced his forearms at the sides of her head, then met her open, unguarded gaze that let him glimpse a part of her huge heart and gentle soul, he realized he wanted this woman most of all. Not the sex. Not her virginity. Not as a conquest or an act of revenge. He just wanted *her*. In his life. Every single fucking day.

The realization hit him like a sucker punch. It was an impossible wish, he knew, because she wasn't his to keep and there was too much pain and past destruction due to her father's actions for them to have any kind of future together. The thought gutted him, and he pushed it aside, focusing instead on the woman in his arms right now.

The sensitive head of his cock was already fitted against the slick opening of her body, and he flexed his hips, slowly working his way inside her, feeling her channel stretch to accommodate his width. Just a few inches in, and her eyes flared wide with shock at the intense pressure of him filling her. She sucked in a quick breath, tensing beneath him, which caused her inner muscles to constrict around his shaft like a little vise of pleasure.

He groaned raggedly, and even though she was incredibly wet and his dick was already coated with her slick moisture, he had to resist the urge to thrust hard and fast and deep and bury himself to the hilt in all that tight heat. Instead, with a tenderness he wasn't even aware he possessed when it came to sex with a woman, he brushed strands of hair away from her flushed face and held her gaze, despite the fact that his blood was on fucking fire.

"Are you okay?" he asked, skimming his thumb along her soft, warm cheek. "If it's too much and you need me to stop—"

"Don't stop," she panted, even though her eyes were glazed over with discomfort. "It burns, but I want more. I want all of you."

Jesus Christ. Her words made him crazy with desire and lust. Need flared through him, hot and unrelenting, and with gritted teeth, he continued to ease his hips forward in slow increments, sinking deeper as Arabella whimpered and writhed beneath him. He came up against a tighter barrier, and she must have realized exactly where he was and what was about to happen, because she wrapped her legs against the backs of his thighs and did her best to keep him from withdrawing even the slightest bit.

She looked up at him with soft, trusting eyes, even though she was tied down and he held all the control. "I don't want you to be gentle or careful, Maddux," she rasped. "Just do it."

He exhaled a harsh breath and pushed his fingers through her hair on either side of her head, holding her immobile. "It's going to hurt, and I'm so fucking sorry."

Knowing there was no easy way to get around the inevitable, he shoved his hips forward in one hard, fast thrust, driving his way past the restricting flesh until every inch of his cock impaled her. She screamed and arched beneath him, and as much as he knew he ought to give her time to adjust to being filled so full, once he was thoroughly encased in all that silken heat, there was no holding back his need to completely claim Arabella and make her his.

It was that primitive thought that urged him to move in and out of her in long, slow, deep strokes that had her body liquifying around his cock and the initial look of pain on her face shifting to something more blissful as her body gradually softened, relaxed, and accepted all of him without any resistance. He maintained a steady rhythm that was more about creating as much pleasure as he could for her given the situation, rather than causing any more pain or discomfort, and in a few minutes' time, she bit her lower lip and started to moan softly, sensually. Her lashes fluttered closed, and her head tipped back as her hips began moving in a natural counterpoint to his lengthening, grinding thrusts.

It was unrealistic to expect her to orgasm the first time he fucked her when she was most likely sore and sensitive, and he figured they had the rest of the night for him to make up for his lack of finesse when his own release was barreling through him at warp speed and he wasn't going to last much longer.

He buried his face against the side of her neck, the rhythm of his pumping hips becoming faster and more erratic. "You feel so fucking good," he groaned into her ear, knowing that things were about to get wilder and rougher than he'd intended with her. "I'm going to come so fucking hard and deep inside you."

"Do it," she urged him huskily, rubbing her cheek against his, her legs wrapping higher and tighter around his waist to lock him close. "I want to feel it. *All* of it."

Jesus fuck. How was it that Arabella was the one bound to his bed, yet she'd somehow managed to steal the control from him with those words and that request that went straight to his cock and hurtled him right over the edge of sanity and straight into a pleasure so electric and intense it overwhelmed his senses?

His shout of satisfaction roared in his ears as his orgasm jolted through him like lightning, triggering jet after jet of semen pulsing along the length of his shaft. Spots danced in front of his eyes, and Maddux's entire body stiffened and jerked uncontrollably as Arabella's tight body milked every last bit of come from his dick.

With a low, guttural groan, Maddux wondered how, after spending all of his adult life without experiencing the taste of heaven on earth Arabella had just given him, he was going to give up this woman when the time came to let her go.

He didn't have a choice, he reminded himself. Despite their agreement, despite taking her virginity, she wasn't his to keep and never would be.

CHAPTER EIGHTEEN

ARABELLA STRUGGLED AT work the following day. She struggled not to yawn at inopportune times because she'd gotten only a fraction of her normal sleep since she'd been otherwise distracted. She struggled to keep her mind on the archiving tasks at hand when her thoughts kept drifting to her erotic night with Maddux and all the places she was now tender as a result of finally relinquishing her V-card to a very well-endowed man. She found herself daydreaming about dawn, when she'd awakened to her new lover spooning her from behind, his hard pillar of flesh prodding her ass as he kissed and nuzzled her neck and fondled her breasts.

She bit her bottom lip to hold in a groan as those hot, arousing memories filled her head and intruded on her concentration. Considering how sore she'd been after her first time with Maddux, there had been no way she could have accommodated his morning wood. But when she'd asked him to show her how to pleasure him with her mouth, he'd been more than willing to teach her what he liked best, and she'd been an enthusiastic student. Between his dirty, filthy words as he'd coached her to suck him off and the way his hand fisted in her hair as he'd guided the rhythm and depth of her mouth along the length of his shaft, her own body had throbbed with renewed desire.

It was all the things she'd imagined oral sex with him to be like, which she'd fantasized about since the morning he'd told her to get on her knees in the kitchen . . . right before they'd been interrupted.

She'd moaned with delight around his cock, and with him reclining against the headboard and her positioned between his spread legs, he'd had a direct view of his dick sliding past her wet lips, her opening as wide as she could and doing her best to swallow him, and learning to relax her gag reflexes when he hit the back of her throat. The last part hadn't been easy, but with him buried as deep as he could go in her mouth, and his hand holding the back of her head in place, she'd learned quickly to breathe through her nose and not choke on the head of his dick.

Hearing him groan and feeling his big body shudder in pleasure as she licked and sucked and savored his cock completely turned her on, too. Made her so restless and enflamed she felt as though she could orgasm without a touch.

"You like sucking me off, don't you, sweet, filthy girl?" he'd murmured as he eased back to let her catch her breath before sliding his shaft right back in again, forcing himself a little deeper.

With her mouth full, she'd whimpered her reply and cast her eager gaze up to his so he could see for himself how much she enjoyed pleasing him, how much she loved sharing something so hot and erotic and intimate with him.

"Finger your pussy," he'd ordered gruffly, and she'd gladly obeyed.

Her hand moved down between her thighs, her fingers sliding through flesh already so slick and needy she almost jumped at the contact. Her clit was swollen and stiff and aching, and she knew it would only take a few firm strokes to make herself climax.

"Don't you dare fucking come until I do," he growled, his amber eyes rimmed with a fiery gold and his features etched with lust as he flexed his hips, reminding her who was in charge and shifting her attention back to the slow, wicked drag of his cock along her tongue and the insistent press of his hand against the back of her head as he pushed all the way back in.

Stroking her drenched folds and bringing herself to the edge of orgasm, then backing off before it completely consumed her was the sweetest kind of torture. And as her desire grew, as her need for release clawed at her restraint, she doubled her efforts to get him off, sucking him more greedily, more deeply, more eagerly, already knowing his climax would directly trigger hers.

His breathing grew choppy and erratic. Beneath the hand she'd placed on his thigh, she felt his muscles tense. His hips jerked, and he groaned as the thick vein in his cock pulsed against her tongue, and the hot, male taste of him flooded her mouth.

She rubbed her clitoris, finally allowing herself to hit that peak, too, her body convulsing and inarticulate sounds vibrating along her vocal cords as she tried to keep up with the steady stream of his come hitting the back of her throat.

"Fuuccckk," he yelled, his voice hoarse as his hips instinctively surged up toward her mouth with each ongoing spurt. "*Suck and swallow*, Bella."

God, *she had*, so deep and so hard, until there was nothing left but his harsh breathing filling his bedroom, and both of their orgasms slowly receded and left them satisfied and awash with physical bliss.

Afterward, they'd shared a shower and breakfast, and he'd shocked her by kissing her before leaving for the MadX-Tech offices for the day. The way his mouth seduced hers had been slower and sweeter than his normal bold, aggressive approach, and while experiencing that affectionate side of Maddux made her heart melt, she knew not to read too much into that romantic gesture so she didn't set herself up for disappointment.

Sex with Maddux had definitely forged an intimacy between them, but she also knew how easily something else could shatter the fragile truce between them. Until things were resolved with her father, she had no idea where she *really* stood with Maddux or if there was any chance that she could come to mean more to him than being a pawn in his game of revenge against her dad.

"Hey, are you okay? You look a little flushed."

Startled out of her private thoughts by her boss's voice, Arabella jumped in her chair, banging her knee on an open desk drawer. She winced, hating that she'd been caught daydreaming, to the extent she hadn't even seen or heard David approach her cubicle.

"Sorry," she murmured guiltily as she rubbed the sore spot on her knee just below the hem of her pencil skirt. "I'm just a little distracted today." *Thinking about how amazing it was to finally lose my virginity.*

"I noticed." His brows furrowed in concern, but he didn't question her further and instead placed some printouts on her desk. "Here's those reports you asked for, but it's already after five, so you can archive the information tomorrow. I'll see you in the morning."

"That sounds good," she said, nodding. "Have a good evening."

"You, too, Arabella."

Once David was gone, she shut down her computer, straightened her desk, and prioritized a stack of work she needed to tackle tomorrow. Her phone, which was sitting next to her keyboard, vibrated with a text. When she saw that it was from Maddux, a giddy feeling swirled inside her and she tapped on the message to read it.

Something came up with a client I need to handle in the city, so I won't be home until around seven this evening. Don't wait for me to eat dinner, and there is no need for you to harp at me through the security cameras since I won't be in my office to enjoy your amusing dialogue.

His open communication and bit of humor was an improvement, too. He certainly didn't have to explain his whereabouts to her, and the fact that he'd been thoughtful enough to do so made her smile.

Milo met her outside of her work building to drive her back to Maddux's, and she was grateful when she walked into the lobby and found it empty. No drama from Gavin today, thank goodness, but knowing the other man well, she wouldn't be surprised if he tried yet again to "save" her.

Up in the penthouse, she made herself a grilled chicken salad and poured a glass of the Pinot Noir that she and Maddux had enjoyed the night before with their meal. Afterward, when the kitchen was cleaned up, she headed into the bedroom to change for the evening. She caught sight of the blouse and leggings that Maddux's sister, Tempest, had so graciously loaned her the other day. She'd already washed and folded them, and she decided that she ought to return the clothing and thank Tempest for a kindness she hadn't had to bestow on Arabella, when she was certain the other woman had to harbor some semblance of resentment against Arabella for whatever her father had done to their family.

After picking up the clothes, she headed two floors down to the level marked with a capital T. She wasn't sure if Tempest had her apartment locked out as Maddux sometimes did, and was glad when the elevator chimed her arrival and the doors slid open on the other woman's floor.

As soon as she stepped foot out of the elevator, it hit Arabella that Tempest's place was the opposite of Maddux's. While his penthouse was sleek clean lines and minimal color, his sister had bright hues splashed all over the place, mostly as accent colors. Reds, oranges, yellows . . . they all blended together in a surprisingly tasteful way, and Arabella guessed the interior design of the place was an expression of Tempest's personality, though she didn't know the woman at all. But a person didn't decorate with such vivid and dramatic flair if they didn't have the bold demeanor to match.

"Oh . . . Hi." Tempest's startled voice pulled Arabella's gaze from a colorful, abstract sculpture she'd been admiring to the stunningly beautiful woman walking toward the entryway, her eyes wide with shock to see who her visitor was.

Arabella smiled at Maddux's sister and lifted the items in her hands so Tempest didn't think she was trying to sneak around. "I'm sorry to surprise you, but I wanted to return the clothes you let me borrow. I really appreciate it, since I know it wasn't something you had to do."

"You're welcome." Tempest took the blouse and leggings and gave Arabella a tentative smile. "It was the least I could do considering how things played out Saturday night. You weren't part of the plan . . . and as much as Hunter and I are trying to understand Maddux's decisions with everything that was at stake, I'm not going to blame you for the things your father has done to my family."

There was a hint of compassion in Tempest's voice toward Arabella that made her attempt to forge a rapport between them. "I have no idea what my father has done, but I know it had to have been something awful for Maddux to go to such extremes. My father won't tell me the truth, and neither will Maddux. It's very frustrating, actually, and I'd really appreciate it if you'd enlighten me."

Tempest hesitated a moment, as if she was considering how much to reveal, then gave her a head a small shake. "I can't. I won't. As much as I'd like to tell you every horrific thing your father and Gavin did to my parents, it's not my place. I don't know why Maddux accepted your proposition instead of just finishing off your father like we all agreed upon, so whatever is between you and my brother, it's up to him to resolve the situation and decide how it's going to all play out."

Arabella tried not to let her dissatisfaction

show, though it was hard to fault Tempest for being loyal to her brother and trusting his choices so completely, even if Tempest didn't agree with or like the decisions he'd made.

"Is my brother treating you okay?" she asked, her tone more curious than concerned. "I know he can be a little . . . okay, a *lot* overbearing and moody, but beneath that gruff exterior, he's really not such a bad guy. He just carries a lot of burden and responsibilities on those big shoulders of his, more than I think is necessary, but that's always been Maddy," she added affectionately. "Especially after losing our parents when we were all so young. He's always been strong and controlled and driven to the extent that sometimes I feel as though he's missing out on the really important things in life."

She didn't elaborate on what she thought those important things were, but Arabella assured Tempest of her original question. "He's been very good to me . . . considering the circumstances. He's a decent and upstanding man, and from what I see and know, he's struggling right now between good versus evil."

Tempest arched a brow in surprise as she held the clothes against her chest. "Wow . . . for you to say that, my brother must have given you a rare glimpse of the kinder, gentler man beneath his surly disposition. I'm shocked . . . I never thought he'd ever willingly expose that vulnerable part of himself to a woman. I mean, as his sister, *I* know it exists because I've seen that side of him, but the only people he's really lowered his guard with are me and Hunter."

Arabella felt her cheeks grow warm as she realized that they were suddenly having a woman-to-woman conversation, that Maddux's sister was intuitive enough to understand that there was something more between Arabella and Maddux... without coming outright and saying it. She wasn't approving, but she wasn't disapproving, either, and Arabella was grateful that Tempest wasn't ostracizing her. And that she didn't hate her for her father's actions.

"If what I sense is true between the two of you," Tempest went on insightfully, a smile touching the corner of her mouth, "all I can say is try and be patient with Maddux. He doesn't let people get close and I'd really hate to see him miss out on the one thing he's never allowed himself to have. Ever."

Arabella didn't know why Tempest was so accepting of her, but it spoke to the kind of woman she was. Forgiving. Soft-hearted. Understanding. At least when it came to her eldest sibling.

"Thank you," Arabella said, not ready to share her own emotions when it came to how she felt about Maddux. Just because she was falling hard for him didn't mean he felt the same at all, and she was smart enough to keep that thought in the forefront in her mind.

After Arabella's interesting conversation with Tempest, she headed back up to Maddux's floor. A glance at the time on her cell phone told her that he should be home soon, and she couldn't contain the anticipation of seeing him and spending time with him.

Arriving on his level, she walked out of the elevator and toward the living room, surprised to find Hunter standing over by the floor-to-ceiling windows overlooking the city. He turned around, and when he saw it was her, a sneer formed on his lips right before he downed the rest of the amber liquid in the glass he held. He'd clearly arrived after she'd gone to Tempest's place, and who knew how many glasses of alcohol he'd already consumed, but judging by the resentful look he cast Arabella's way, things didn't bode well for her.

This Wilder sibling wasn't as benevolent or compassionate as his sister had just been. No, there was loathing in his eyes as he raked his contemptuous gaze down the length of her, then back up again.

"Ahhh, Maddux's kept woman," he said caustically as he set his empty glass on the living room table and slowly strolled toward where she was standing, stopping a few feet away. "What is it about you that's gotten under my brother's skin? That he'd so carelessly throw away fucking *years* of planning for a woman he should despise just as much as her father?"

The anger in his voice was palpable, and Arabella lifted her chin and held her ground. "Whatever my father did, I had no part of."

"No, of course you didn't," he drawled in a patronizing tone, close enough now that she could smell the alcohol on his breath. "But that doesn't change the fact that you're Theodore's blood, and you're probably just as conniving as your father and you're trying to mess with my brother's head. But make no mistake, Arabella Cole. You're nothing more than a harlot to him. A whore that he's going to get tired of, and then he'll get his shit together and finish what your father started and drag both Gavin and Theodore down to the depths of hell, where they fucking belong."

Arabella's hands clutched into fists at her sides at Hunter's derogatory remark, and keeping her own temper in check took effort. "Even though you deserve to be slapped across the face for your rude comment about me, I'm going to let it slide because you're clearly drunk and angry."

"Why the fuck shouldn't I be angry?" he yelled, loud and belligerent. "Your goddamn father *killed* our parents."

Arabella gasped, feeling as though all the oxygen had suddenly been sucked out of the room. Shock kept her entire body rooted to the spot, and she prayed that somehow, someway, she'd misheard Hunter. "What did you say?"

"I said, your prick of a father killed my mother and father," he said, his voice calmer but no less harsh. "All because he was so fucking greedy he extorted monthly payments from small businesses like my parents' diner. And when they were so tapped out financially and couldn't pay what Theodore demanded, he decided to teach them a lesson that cost both of them their lives."

The horrifying image that Hunter painted in Arabella's mind caused hot tears to fill her eyes. "You have to be mistaken," she rasped. She didn't want to believe it. She was beginning to think her father was capable of many illegal and criminal activities, but *murder*? She was having a difficult time wrapping her mind around the possibility, but if it was true, then oh, God . . .

A sob escaped her throat, her heart felt as though it was splintering in two, and all she could think was that she had to confront her father, face-to-face. She desperately *needed* straight answers. No more evading her questions. No more lies. She had to look in his eyes and know if he was really capable of ending two innocent people's lives.

She spun around and rushed toward the elevator.

"Where are you going?" Hunter demanded.

He sounded so much like Maddux in that moment—authoritative and as though his voice alone ought to halt her in her tracks. But unlike his brother's commands, Hunter's brusque tone did nothing to dissuade Arabella. She had no loyalty to Hunter, and wasn't this what he wanted? Her out of his brother's life?

"I'm going to find out the truth from my father," she said, her voice a shredded wreck. "I need to hear it from him because I can't believe he'd do something so horrific." Or rather, she didn't *want* to believe it, but the churning in her stomach was not a good omen.

"Arabella, stop," Hunter said, more forcefully this time.

She ignored him, her gaze going to the numbers above the elevator doors that indicated that someone was using the lift and heading to the upper floors. Feeling unsettled and anxious and upset, she decided she wasn't going to wait around for the elevator to arrive when there was an alternate route that would get her to the lobby, then out to the main street, much quicker. And from there, once she was out of the building, she'd either catch a cab or call an Uber to take her to her father's place in the city.

Hearing Hunter's footsteps behind her and not wanting to give him the chance to stop her from leaving, she darted down the side hallway and pushed out the emergency exit door that led to a stairwell. His string of curses hit her ears just as the door slammed shut behind her and she raced down the spiral of stairs until she burst free into the lobby, ran out the main doors of the building, and headed down the street toward the next block.

Once and for all, Arabella wasn't going to let up on her father until she knew everything, even if it was painful for her to hear—and dear God, she was expecting the worst. Because when her relationship with her father flashed through her mind, she realized she'd spent so many years away from home in boarding school and college. What did she really know about him, his business, and what he did outside of the idyllic home life he'd created for the two of them?

She hadn't known about her father's gambling addiction or the astronomical debt he'd accumulated, or the fact that he'd willingly signed all his assets over to what had been the equivalent of a loan shark. They'd been living a *lie* and she hadn't even known, and the possibility that her father was cold and calculating enough to extort money from small businesses—as Hunter had claimed— to possibly feed his gambling issue or fund their lavish lifestyle made her nauseous.

Cars drove along the street, but there were no cabs to hail. Keeping a fast walk, she unlocked her phone and pressed on the Uber app to request a ride, and right before she completed the process, a black Mercedes with tinted windows came to a stop a few feet ahead of her along the curb. The back door opened right in front of where she was walking, and before she could skirt around it, a man she didn't recognize stepped out, grabbed her arm, and yanked her back into the vehicle with him.

It all happened so fast she didn't even have time to scream. But she did hear Maddux yell her name right before the door slammed shut and the car merged back into the flow of traffic, leaving her sitting next to a scary-looking man with a jagged scar slashed across his face, and ice-cold fear running through her veins.

CHAPTER NINETEEN

CONSIDERING THE OUTSTANDING way his meeting in the city had gone with *ethical* law enforcement officials, Maddux ought to be in a fucking fantastic mood. Instead, as he parked his car in his designated spot in the underground parking structure and headed into the lobby of his building, dread settled like a ten-ton weight on his chest because his elation was coming at the steep cost of ripping Arabella's entire world apart.

But there was no stopping the wheels that had been set in motion for what was going to take place tomorrow, and as much as he'd come to care for Arabella—more than he'd ever believed was possible—he'd already disappointed his brother and sister once, and letting them down again wasn't an option. He'd promised them both that he'd make things right, and he refused to let this golden opportunity slip through his fingers when Theodore and Gavin deserved to rot in hell.

Or in this case, in prison. Possibly, for the rest of their lives.

Maddux wearily scrubbed a hand along the light scrape of beard covering his jawline, honestly wishing that he'd met Arabella under better, more normal circumstances, instead of taking her in exchange for her father's debt. Maybe things would have ended up differently for them, but he'd never know and he wouldn't dwell on the recent past. What was done was done, and after he sat down with her tonight and revealed what was going to happen to her father tomorrow, she was going to hate his fucking guts and never want to see him again. He was sure of it.

It was time he told Arabella *everything* so she understood his reasons for going to the lengths he had to bring Theodore to his knees. Securing her father's debt and assets had only been a small preview to Theodore's destruction. What no one else knew, not even his brother or sister, was that Maddux had spent years and hundreds of thousands of dollars in resources trying to build a solid case against Theodore and Gavin for their criminal activities.

What he hadn't expected was all the corrupt political representatives and law enforcement agents who had road blocked Maddux's many attempts to get the duo arrested... because as Maddux had uncovered, the case against Theodore and Gavin was much bigger than just the two of them. With a whole lot of insistent digging, he'd learned that Addingwell Financial—where they and many others were "employed"—was actually a front for organized crime.

A lot of palms throughout the local, state, and

federal agencies were being greased on a regular basis to deflect the heat off of their illegal activities. Those bribes and hush money were also keeping the higher-ranking Mafioso untouchable. The cesspool of fraud, nepotism, and misrepresentation Maddux had encountered over the years had sickened him, and it wasn't until very recently that he'd found a reputable group of attorneys who were just as eager to bring down the organization as Maddux was, and who helped in breaking the case wide open.

For months, Maddux didn't think it was going to happen, which was why he'd kept everything close to his vest. But it had been a matter of persistence and weeding their way through all the obstruction to finally get the attention of the ethical agents within the FBI.

And now, as of tomorrow morning, there would be over a dozen raids and arrests all over the city, and Theodore and Gavin were on that list.

Reaching the lobby elevator, Maddux stepped inside the lift and pressed the button for his penthouse, then took off his suit jacket and tugged at the tie around his neck to give the material some slack so it didn't feel like a noose strangling him. With each upward level he passed, the knot in his stomach tightened. This wasn't the way he wanted things to end between himself and Arabella after everything they'd shared in a very short time, but she would undoubtedly find his actions unforgivable. And a part of him understood the anger and resentment she was going to feel toward him . . . an ironic situation when he and his siblings had lived the past fourteen years feeling the same way about her father.

The elevator chimed as he reached his floor, and after the doors slid open and he stepped out, he heard the emergency stairway door slam shut, which was odd since nobody used that exit unless, well, there was an emergency. He shifted his gaze to his brother, who was standing only a few feet away, an abnormal look of panic and dismay flashing across his features.

"Fuck!" Hunter said, and jammed his hands through his hair, pulling on the strands in agitation. "I'm sorry . . . I'm so goddamn sorry!"

Confusion filtered through Maddux, and he tried not to let his brother's rattled composure worry him until he found out what had caused it. Hard to tell with Hunter lately, since his behavior had been running hot and cold since the night of the ball. Maddux wasn't sure if it was a result of everything that had, or rather hadn't, gone down with Theodore or the fact that the woman Hunter had met and slept with ditched him without a trace.

"Sorry for what?" Maddux asked calmly as he dropped his suit jacket on the back of the nearest chair in the living room. "What's going on and who was that that just went out the stairwell?"

"It was Arabella," Hunter blurted out. "I

came up here to talk to you, then she arrived and I said some things out of pent-up anger and I told her about her father killing our parents. She didn't believe me and was insistent she talk to her father, and she ran out."

Maddux's entire body tensed and he tried to hold back the fury rising up in him. He'd wanted everything with Arabella to come out in a controlled environment, and in a way that he could soften whatever he could, and not just yell out the fact that her father and Gavin were murderers without giving her the whole, complete picture.

He jabbed a finger toward his brother. "You had no right to tell her," he said heatedly.

Hunter went from apologetic to defensive in a hot second. "I had *every* right because she needs to know what a prick her father is. And *you* weren't going to tell her, so I did!"

Maddux felt torn, because a part of him understood his brother's fury, while another part of him wanted to protect Arabella from... everything.

"She's not what you think," Maddux said, his voice dropping to a low growl. Arabella was soft and gentle and sweet. And so fucking crushable when it came to her emotions. "She's nothing like her father, and so help me God, if anything happens to her as a result of her running out of here, I am going to kick your ass for letting her go."

Hunter gaped at him. "Are you fucking serious?"

"Dead serious." Yes, at the moment, he was choosing sides. He was choosing to go after Arabella, making it clear to his brother that she was more than just a pawn to him. And trying to explain his feelings to Hunter was impossible when he'd never felt like this toward any other woman.

But all that was eclipsed by a rush of fear . . . that something might happen to her once she ran out of the building and was no longer under his protection. Once she was with her father, or with Gavin, who Maddux didn't trust with a ten-foot pole. The other man was a user, an abuser, and when it came to Arabella, Gavin wouldn't hesitate to use her for leverage, to avoid his arrest tomorrow.

Maddux had to get to Arabella first. Not wanting to waste any more time arguing with his brother, he ran for the stairs and jumped over the handrails to make his way down to the lobby twice as fast, but when he arrived, Arabella was already gone. He bolted for the main doors, and once he was out on the sidewalk, he glanced down the street just as a black Mercedes came to a stop by Arabella.

As soon as Maddux saw a guy open the back door and realized what was about to happen, panic twisted through his entire being as he rushed toward her. "Arabella!" he yelled, but she was too far away for him to reach in time, and the other man yanked her inside the car so fast and so rough she never had a chance to fight him off.

Then the car was driving away as Maddux's worst fears were realized. She'd been kidnapped, snatched right off the street by the kind of guy who looked more like a mercenary than a friendly citizen offering her a ride. He had no idea where that car was taking her or what fate awaited her once she arrived, but his gut was screaming at him that she was heading straight toward something, or someone, dangerous.

Maddux ran back into his building, guilt already twisting through him for failing her, for not being able to get to Arabella before someone else had grabbed her. The spike of adrenaline surging through his veins made his heart race at an alarming speed, but it also gave him the strength to power back up the stairs to his penthouse in less than a minute.

He needed to make a call to authorities, the ones he'd been working with and who were preparing for tomorrow's arrests. As far as Maddux was concerned, Arabella's abduction changed everything, and he'd pay whatever it cost to any agency to make finding her a priority.

He would tear this fucking city apart until he knew she was safe and, hopefully, unharmed. He wouldn't be able to live with the guilt and soul-deep pain if anything horrible happened to her, and he refused to think that anything would before he found her.

CHAPTER TWENTY

"I KNEW IF we waited long enough the opportunity to grab you would eventually happen."

The man sitting with Arabella in the back seat of the Mercedes smirked at her, looking pleased with himself. Despite the luxurious Mercedes they were being chauffeured in, the guy looked like a hoodlum with his greasy hair, stained teeth, and that jagged scar on his face. Based on his comment, he must have been watching her for a while now, but up until her leaving the building this evening on her own, she'd always been with Milo. She'd made herself an easy target, but for whom?

She did her best to keep her fear in check, because she refused to show this man any weakness. "Who are you and what do you want?"

"Who I am doesn't matter," he said nonchalantly as he unlocked his phone and pressed a button to make a call. "What do I want? Payment for delivering you to the man who hired me to take you."

"What man?" she asked, though she had a

sinking feeling she already knew. This scheme had Gavin written all over it.

"Not for me to say." He put the phone to his ear, waited a few beats, then spoke to whoever picked up the line. "It's done. We have her. ETA in ten minutes."

He disconnected the call, and Arabella was at least grateful that he stayed to his side of the back seat. Clearly, the money awaiting him was far more enticing than messing around with her. "Where are you taking me?"

He smirked at her. "It's a surprise."

Asshole. Arabella took note of her surroundings as the car drove to the outskirts of the city, the direct opposite of Gavin's place, or even her father's, which she found disconcerting. She still had her cell phone, and keeping it down low near her door, she tried to swipe it open so she could at least try to text Maddux to reassure him that she was okay. Or at least she was for the moment.

"Don't do it," the guy next to her said, his voice sharp with warning. "Put your phone on your lap so I can see it, along with your hands."

Not wanting to test him, she did as she was told, though she was surprised that he hadn't confiscated the device. A few minutes later, they arrived in a lower-income neighborhood and pulled up to a house that was clearly in need of repair. The garage door opened for them when they turned into the driveaway, and the man in the front seat of the car pulled into the space. A moment later, the garage door sealed shut behind them, and Arabella swallowed back the apprehension threatening to overwhelm her.

Scar Face opened his door, slid out, and glanced down at her. "Out," he ordered, indicating with a hand motion that she was to vacate the vehicle from his side of the car, not her own.

She slid across the seat, and as soon as she was standing in the dark, dank garage, he grabbed her arm and pushed her toward a door that opened as they approached. Standing on the threshold was Gavin. She couldn't say she was shocked, but she had no idea why he'd bring her to such a dilapidated place, and that's what concerned her the most.

Once she was shoved into the house and into an outdated kitchen that needed a major overhaul, Gavin and the other man made a quick monetary exchange. Payment for her delivery out of the way, Gavin closed and locked the door with an interior key before turning to face her, an insolent smile on his face as he brandished a gun from the back waistband of his pants.

She sucked in a startled breath as he pointed it directly at her, showing her he meant business. Fear wrapped itself around her, but the last thing she wanted to show Gavin was weakness. But seeing him with a gun directed at her? Jesus, her heart was racing a mile a minute.

"Ahhh, Arabella," he said in a smooth, calm, almost affectionate tone. "So nice of you to join me here."

She narrowed her gaze at him, a little unnerved by his weird behavior, not to mention having no idea what he intended. "I was kidnapped right off the street by a shady-looking man. You didn't give me much of a choice *but* to join you here."

It was like watching the flip of a switch as Gavin went from civil to antagonistic. "And Maddux isn't giving me much of a choice, either," he snapped.

She had no idea what he was referring to. Or what would make him feel the need to direct the barrel of a gun at her. "What are you talking about?"

Gavin inclined his head toward an area with an old, beat-up couch and two worn wooden chairs. "Come with me into the living room so we can have a little chat."

When she didn't move, he nudged her in the side with the weapon, forcing her to walk in that direction. Trying desperately to keep her panic at bay, she followed him into another room. The curtains were drawn over all the windows, and while there was one lamp on, it was dark and felt very secluded inside the house. From what she could tell, the two of them were alone, which kicked up her anxiety a few notches.

"What is this place?" she asked, turning around to face him again. She still held her cell phone, but she tried her best to keep it out of sight. It was the only lifeline she had. "And why would you bring me here?"

He gave her a grin that seemed borderline psychotic. "Why, you're my catnip to lure the beast to his demise."

He was beginning to sound like a madman in a cartoon except this was real life and that gun probably had very real bullets. Knowing she needed to keep calm and buy time, she kept talking. "Why do you want Maddux here?" She shook her head in confusion. "Because of the debt and asset situation?" It was the only thing that made sense, but his tactic seemed extreme.

"No, that's your father's petty issue with Maddux," Gavin said as he picked up the bottle of whiskey off a small wooden table and poured himself a generous amount. "My problem with that asshole is *much* bigger than that. You see, it's been brought to my attention that he's digging around in places that he shouldn't and that aren't any of his fucking business."

He was talking in riddles. "Digging around in *what* places?"

"The organization your father and I work for." He took a long swallow of the alcohol and didn't so much as wince as the fiery liquid made its way to his stomach.

She frowned, trying to make some kind of sense of what he was saying. "You mean Addingwell Financial?" Why would Maddux concern himself with the company Gavin and her father worked for?

Gavin exhaled a long-suffering sigh, as if he was dealing with someone dense. "It's all a front, Ari. For organized crime. Your father and I have always worked for the mafia, and Maddux has taken it upon himself to make it his fucking crusade to expose and take down the organization. He's been at it for years, but now he's getting close to threatening my livelihood, and it's time to get rid of him for good. And this hellhole is a little investment I made just for this occasion. A few gunshots in this part of the neighborhood won't be a cause for concern."

Arabella's stomach cramped at the realization of just how serious Gavin was about his threat against Maddux and his deranged plans to kill him. "Where is my father?" she demanded, doing everything she could to beat back the fear clawing at her insides. "Does he know about me being here? He couldn't have agreed to any of this."

Gavin tossed back the rest of the whiskey and slammed the empty glass down on the table, making Arabella jump from the sharp noise in the too quiet house. "Yes, your father knows you're here," he said, his eyes glazing over as the considerable amount of alcohol he'd just consumed in such a short period of time started making its way through his system. "No, I can't say that he agreed to this plan of mine. In fact, he was adamantly *against* it, but he's an old man who no longer has the capacity to do the kind of dirty work that needs to get done in this business. He's gone all soft on me and has decided to grow a conscience, despite all the blood he already has on his hands." Disgust laced Gavin's voice.

"And as for where he is . . ." He walked over to what looked like a coat closet and unlatched the lock securing it closed. "Well, he's already here, actually. Why don't we have him join the party?"

Gavin opened the door, and seeing wooden stairs heading down to a dark lower level, Arabella realized that they led to a basement.

"Get up here, old man," Gavin called out, his tone rude to a man who'd always been good to him.

Arabella was shocked that Gavin had locked up her father, when her dad had treated him as the equivalent of a son for so many years. With Gavin's current agenda, which her father didn't seem to agree with, that relationship had swiftly changed.

"Oh, and I'll take your cell phone for safekeeping," Gavin said, eyeing the device she still held in her hand, which she reluctantly handed over, leaving her with no means to contact the outside world.

She heard shuffling on the stairs, then her father appeared and stepped into the living room. His hair was in disarray around his head, his face was pale and drawn, and his eyes held a wealth of remorse as they met hers. His normally neat and pressed clothes were a rumpled mess. Her heart leapt into her throat. Good God, how long had he been down there?

"Dad!" she cried out and rushed to him, pulling him into her embrace, hating that he felt so frail in her arms. Despite everything, he was still her father and she loved him. "What's going on?" she asked, once she was looking into his eyes again.

Her father glared at the other man in the room, who oh so casually kept his gun directed their way. "Gavin is on a bit of a power trip. He seems to think that taking out Maddux is going to make the investigation of Addingwell Financial and the organization disappear."

"Maybe. Maybe not," Gavin said with a shrug. "But killing Maddux will give me a *great* sense of satisfaction. He's been a fucking thorn in our side for years, the condescending bastard. Now, as for the two of you, move over to those wooden chairs, and Arabella, take one of those plastic zip ties and secure your father's feet together, then his hands. Once that's done, sit down in the other chair and do your own feet."

With the weapon still in Gavin's hand, along with his growing agitation, Arabella didn't argue. She knelt in front of her father and secured his ankles with shaking hands before doing his wrists, too.

"Are you okay?" she asked in concern as she worked at her task. "Is your heart good?"

"Yeah, yeah, yeah," Gavin interrupted in an annoyed tone as he waved the gun in the air. "Your old man already had an angina attack when I first brought him here. Luckily he has his nitroglycerin pills on him, or he might have died."

Gavin sounded like he didn't care one way or another, and Arabella wondered when he'd gotten so coldhearted. He'd always been an arrogant jerk, but this callous man was one she'd never seen or encountered before, and she'd be lying if she said that his apathetic attitude didn't scare her. Especially since he was drinking and had a gun in his hand. God only knew what he had planned.

"I'm good, Arabella," her father said in a low voice, and still on her knees in front of him, Arabella lifted her gaze to his weary, pain-filled eyes as he spoke. "I'm so sorry. I never wanted you to get caught up in all this. I always tried to keep my job separate from our relationship because I never wanted you to think any less of me."

She had no response to that as she sat in her own chair and tightened the strip of plastic around her ankles as instructed while Gavin watched to make sure she didn't leave the ties too loose. Did she think any less of her father? The question was a deeply agonizing one, because while she'd once put him up on a pedestal, he'd definitely taken a long fall from grace in her eyes just on the basis of who he worked for and what he did for a living. Her father was involved with the mafia, and she could only imagine the illegal activities he'd been involved in—most of which had probably funded his gambling addiction and the debt that had snowballed. Not to mention what he'd done to make the Wilder siblings hate him so much.

As soon as Gavin secured her hands, Arabella placed them on her lap and glanced at her father, whose head hung in shame. "Is it true that you killed Maddux's parents?" she asked. The question came out on a raw rasp, and she was so afraid to hear the answer, even though she already knew the truth in her gut.

Her dad met her gaze, a flicker of regret in the depths. "It was an accident."

"It wasn't a fucking accident!" Gavin refuted with a deranged laugh. "Tell her the truth, Theodore. You ordered me to set that grease fire that night at the diner, knowing full well that Maddux's mother was in the back office, and Maddux and his father were on their way to the restaurant to pick her up after closing time."

Her father shook his head. "It was just meant to scare them so they'd pay what they owed me," he said defensively. "They weren't supposed to die."

Was he honestly trying to justify their deaths? "Paid what they *owed* you?" Arabella repeated incredulously, recalling what Hunter had told her earlier that had prompted her to run. "You *extorted* money from them and from other businesses."

"That's what we do, Arabella," Gavin said with a shrug. "The organization gets a percentage, and we get a nice little cut to supplement our income. And if we have to get our hands dirty every so often to keep everyone in line, then so be it."

"That's disgusting." And so heartbreaking, when she thought of all the people her father and Gavin had hurt, swindled . . . or killed. Her mouth grew dry and her stomach pitched with nausea.

"Yeah, well, as cozy as this kumbaya moment is, you're both wasting my time. Now, all we're missing is the guest of honor to this fun little party," he said, an eager gleam in eyes. "As soon as Maddux knows I've kidnapped you, it'll just be a matter of a very short time before he arrives to save his precious Bella."

"He's not going to come for me," she insisted, trying to divert Gavin's plan, or else Maddux would be walking right into an ambush. "I'm worth nothing to him."

"Nice try," he said, pacing in front of their two chairs. "I saw the interaction between the two of you when I was there for the welfare check. He certainly didn't act as though he hated you, and you were very eager to stay with him. In fact, I'm betting he's already fucked you, which is a shame because you really should have been mine, and now you're just used goods."

"I'll *never* be yours," she spat, her hatred toward Gavin at an all-time high.

"This is true, considering how tonight is going to end." He lifted her phone, swiped open the screen, and scrolled through her contacts. "Ahh, here he is, under *The Beast*. How charming," he said, sarcasm coating his words. "Now, let's test that theory about whether or not Maddux will come to your rescue."

"*Arabella's life for yours*," Gavin said out loud as he typed the words into a text message, his voice almost gleeful at the high of having what he believed was the upper hand. "*What's it going to be, Wilder?*"

Less than fifteen seconds later, her phone rang, and Gavin looked at the display and smirked as he answered the call, put it on speakerphone, and spoke. "Well, that didn't take long. I think maybe Arabella misjudged your affection for her. Her life for yours, Wilder. I think that's a fair trade."

"How about *your* life for hers, you son of a bitch!" Maddux's deep, furious voice rang out like thunder. "I'm already on my way to your shitty hideout. I had a tracker put on Arabella's phone, just in case something like this happened."

"How resourceful," Gavin drawled. "If you bring the cops with you, she dies before you even step foot inside the door."

Arabella sucked in a sharp breath. Jesus, Gavin was truly insane, she thought, real fear settling in her bones.

"I'll be alone," Maddux bit out. "And if you

fucking hurt her, *you* will die a slow, very painful death."

Arabella's heart was racing wildly in her chest, pumping panic through her veins, because she knew if Maddux arrived, he'd be nothing more than a dead man walking. That was Gavin's entire plan.

"Don't come here, Maddux," she yelled out, loud enough for him to hear. "It's a trap!"

Fury raged across Gavin's features at her warning to Maddux, and he lifted the gun and pointed it right between her eyes, making her blood freeze in her veins at the thought of him pulling the trigger. "Shut the fuck up," he shouted.

"Gavin, stop," her father pleaded, his voice wheezing. "This is going too far!"

Ignoring Theodore, Gavin exhaled a deep breath, trying to regain his composure before speaking into the phone again. "Ten minutes, Wilder. That's all you've got before I start putting holes in your girl."

He disconnected the call, and while he lowered the weapon, his dark, angry glare remained on Arabella.

She jutted out her chin, no longer caring if she irritated him or not. What did she have to lose? "You won't get away with this, Gavin."

"Ahhh, that's where you're wrong, Arabella," he said, his dark, hatred-filled gaze focusing on her. "I've worked too fucking hard to get to where I am, and no one, not you, your father, or Maddux, is going to fuck it up for me. Which means tonight is all about eliminating anything and everything standing in my way . . . which is all *three* of you. And once you're all dead, I'm going to burn this place down so there is nothing left except all of your ashes."

Gavin's rant was crazy and insane, but the most frightening thing of all was that Arabella believed every word he said.

CHAPTER TWENTY-ONE

Maddux's stomach rolled as he broke every speed limit in the vicinity to get to the address that had shown up on the tracker he'd installed on Arabella's phone the first night she'd spent at his place. He hadn't been worried about her escaping, not when she'd given herself up for her father's debt so willingly. No, the added security had given him peace of mind as to her safety at all times. He didn't trust Gavin and knew the possibility existed that he might try and kidnap Arabella out of spite and to piss Maddux off.

His instincts had been accurate on one account . . . Gavin *had* provoked him to the point of rage, and the fact that he was using Arabella as leverage to lure Maddux in only made him feel twice as violent toward the other man. Without any hesitation or doubts, Maddux would voluntarily sacrifice his life for Arabella's . . . but he was determined to make sure they both walked out of this situation alive.

He tried not to think about the tumult of emotions tightening in his chest, the ones that told him that Arabella meant so much more to him than the revenge he'd sought the night of the fairy-tale ball. Somewhere along the way, this woman had managed to charm him with her wit and smiles and the way she'd let herself be vulnerable with him. She'd gained his respect with her loyalty and somehow eased the anger and resentment he'd carried in his soul the past fourteen years. And even though he'd believed it wasn't possible, she'd thawed the ice around his heart and made him want *more* with her... yet there was so much turmoil between their families, not to mention that by tomorrow her father would be sitting in a jail cell, which Maddux would have played a large part of. He wasn't sure Arabella would ever be able to forgive him for taking down the only parent *she* had left.

But none of that would matter if tonight went to shit, and not knowing what Gavin had planned, Maddux had to prepare himself for any and every possible scenario. As he turned into a low-income, drug-infested neighborhood, he forced himself to calm down, knowing if he rushed in with a hot head and a vicious temper, he wasn't going to be able to think clearly and was liable to make stupid mistakes. He needed his wits about him to assess the situation and to make sure that nothing happened to Arabella.

That was his one and only concern—her safety—because if anything happened to her, he'd never forgive himself, since he'd been the one to start this particular war. Once he'd ensured her freedom from this terrifying situation, then all hell could and would break loose. Reinforcement wasn't far behind him. He'd given himself a good fifteen-minute lead before making the calls that would ensure he'd have backup, but Maddux knew how careful and judicious a SWAT team was when it came to a hostage situation, and he wasn't in the mood to waste hours on a negotiation that probably wouldn't happen anyway.

Arriving at the address, he parked his car in the driveway, got out of his vehicle, and made his way to the front door. The entire front of the house was pitch-dark, and the curtains were drawn across all the windows, which made it look as if no one was home. He rapped his knuckles three times on the door.

"It's Maddux," he said, and a few seconds later, a dim porch light flicked on, and the door opened, with Gavin greeting him with a gun pointed at his chest.

It took every ounce of control that Maddux possessed not to bum-rush Gavin like a fucking linebacker—there was no doubt in his mind he could overpower the other man when Maddux outweighed him in pure muscle by a good thirty pounds. But not knowing what the situation was inside the house, and with Gavin holding a deadly weapon, Maddux needed to be smart and precise about every move he made if he wanted to get himself and Arabella out of this alive.

"Nice to know that chivalry isn't dead," Gavin mocked, a twisted smile on his lips. "Now lift your shirt and turn around so I can make sure you're not hiding any kind of weapon. Then pull up your pant legs, too."

At least he was being thorough, Maddux thought, as he showed the other man what he wanted to see. He'd expected the search and had brought nothing with him weapon-wise... besides his bare hands and a brute strength Gavin was no match for.

Once Gavin was satisfied that Maddux was clean, he opened the door wider and motioned him inside. Keeping his pistol trained on Maddux from a few feet away, he turned off the porch light and relocked the front door.

"Maddux... no," Arabella said, drawing his attention to the adjoining living room, where she and her father sat on two chairs with their hands and feet secured. "You shouldn't have come. He has every intention of killing you and us."

The sound of Arabella's choked voice gripped Maddux, along with the fact that she'd been willing to risk her own life to save his with her warning that this was a trap. It took effort not to react to that fear and anguish in her voice, to reassure her that everything was going to be just fine. Right now, he needed every single bit of his concentration on Gavin and finding the right opportunity to take him down.

"I can't say that Arabella is wrong. Unfortunately, none of you are walking out of here alive tonight." Gavin nodded toward where Arabella and Theodore were tied up. "Come on over here, where I can keep a better eye on all of you until I decide whose life I want to end first."

And shockingly, one of those lives he wanted to cut short included Theodore, and Maddux couldn't help but wonder how the older man had landed himself on the receiving end of Gavin's madness. At the moment, though, the hows and whys didn't matter.

Crossing to the living room, Maddux deliberately positioned himself a few feet away from Arabella's side, but he couldn't bring himself to look at her, because he knew if he looked into her eyes and witnessed her terror and despair for himself, it would gut him, and he couldn't afford the distraction. He saw a bottle of whiskey on a nearby table, a quarter of its contents gone, and hoped Gavin had stupidly consumed the alcohol, which would make his reflexes not as sharp or precise.

"I'm here, just like you asked," Maddux said evenly, keeping his gaze trained on Gavin and wanting the other man's attention solely on him. "I'm the one you want, not Arabella. Let her go."

Gavin laughed, though the sound lacked any humor. "News flash, Wilder. I'm not letting *anyone* go. Theodore and Arabella are nothing more than collateral damage, and you're going to die, because with you no longer poking your nose where it doesn't belong, Addingwell Financial will remain as it is."

Maddux arched a sardonic brow. "A front for organized crime?"

"Yes," Gavin admitted with a shrug. "And I'm thinking once my bosses find out that I'm the one who got rid of you, and your case against the organization falls apart without your deposition or testimony, there'll be a nice promotion in it for me."

"You're crazy to think that's how things will play out," Theodore said, though his voice sounded weak and defeated.

Gavin swung the barrel of his gun toward the older man, a cruel smile on his lips, and Arabella made a small, desperate sound now that her father had grabbed Gavin's attention. "Unfortunately, you won't be around to see what happens or rat me out. And neither will Arabella. I'm not leaving *anything* to chance."

Clearly irritated now, Gavin clenched his jaw. "So, who should be first to die? Such a hard decision." He moved his pistol to Arabella, then glanced at Maddux, a malicious gleam in his eyes. "Then again, maybe not. You deserve to suffer, Wilder, and what's worse than watching someone you care about die right before your eyes?"

A renewed rage pumped through Maddux at the reference Gavin was making, to the night he'd set the grease fire in his parents' diner and Maddux had witnessed his parents' deaths. It had been the single most excruciating thing he'd experienced in his life, and he knew that he wouldn't survive the same fate with Arabella.

Maddux wasn't going to take any chances with her life. Done with this fucker and his mind games, he made a split-second decision, and fueled by pure outrage, he rushed toward the other man. The surprise attack startled Gavin, and just as Maddux intended, the other man shifted his aim to him and pulled the trigger.

Maddux heard Arabella scream his name as an explosion of sound echoed in the room, and an excruciating, searing pain ripped through his right shoulder seconds before he tackled Gavin to the floor. He knew he'd been hit, but the adrenaline surging through his body masked the burn of flesh as he knocked the gun from Gavin's grasp. The other man struggled, but he was no match for Maddux's strength and weight as he secured his arm tight around Gavin's neck in a choke hold until he finally passed out and went limp.

"Maddux," Arabella said, a sob catching in her throat as she dropped to the floor next to him, though her hands and feet were still secured with the plastic ties. "Oh, my God, you've been shot!"

Rolling to his knees, he glanced down at the wet, red stain on his white shirt near his upper shoulder and winced at the agonizing, throbbing ache that was now making itself known. He wasn't gushing blood, which meant a main artery hadn't been severed, the wound wasn't life-threatening, and once he got medical attention, he'd be good as new with a few stitches to add to the scars along his neck.

"It's just a flesh wound. I'll be fine," Maddux assured her, and knowing he only had a few minutes until Gavin regained consciousness, he grabbed a few of the zip ties left on the table and secured the other man's hands and feet.

"You could have been killed," she said, the raw emotion in her voice causing him to stop and focus his attention on *her*.

He needed to get a knife from the kitchen to cut her out of the restraints, but the tears streaming down her face made his heart squeeze like a vise in his chest. He gathered her into his arms to show her that he was okay, that *they* were going to be okay. He held her tight as she buried her face against his neck, more grateful that *she'd* been spared when Gavin clearly intended to kill her first.

She finally lifted her head and looked into his eyes, hers still damp with tears. "If anything happened to you, I'd be devastated."

God, he understood, because he felt the same way.

And then all that hell he'd been waiting for to break loose finally happened as a battering ram busted down the door. SWAT officers rushed in, guns drawn, ending fourteen years of pain, resentment, and Maddux's thirst for revenge.

It was finally over.

Arabella paced back and forth in the hospital's waiting room, feeling weary, exhausted, and utterly drained after the emotional roller coaster she'd been on the past few hours. After being kidnapped off the street, dealing with an unhinged Gavin, and witnessing the horror of Maddux getting shot trying to protect her, she wasn't sure her heart could take much more. On top of that, she'd been a hysterical, crying mess as she'd watched law enforcement escort her father out of the house in handcuffs right after Gavin. As much as she loved her dad, she knew he'd most likely spend the rest of his years behind bars for the crimes he'd committed, and that was a harrowing thought to process.

She swallowed back another rise of tears that threatened to overwhelm her. It was such a sad, heartbreaking situation, and the next few months were going to be difficult as her father was prosecuted and put on trial and most likely found guilty for numerous offenses.

God, it was as though she hadn't known her dad at all. Just the aspects that he'd wanted her to see, or the illusions he'd created to offset who he worked for and what he did for a living. But the fact was, there were horrible things he'd had a hand in, like the death of Maddux's parents, and he needed to atone for those immoral choices he'd made.

As for Gavin... tonight, he'd racked up kidnapping and attempted murder charges to his long list of other felonies. He'd get his day in court, too, and she hoped when the time came, he received the maximum sentence. She never wanted to see him again in her lifetime.

While Maddux had been getting his wound stitched and patched up—thankfully, the bullet had entered and exited cleanly, just below the collarbone—she'd spent the past few hours in the waiting room being interviewed by two FBI agents who'd accompanied them to the hospital, answering what felt like a million questions about the night's events. She'd given them her statement, they'd told her they'd be in touch, and when they were done with her and gotten an all clear from the doctor on Maddux's procedure, they'd gone into his room to take his account of what had happened, too.

The two men had left about twenty minutes ago, and now Arabella was anxiously waiting for her opportunity to see and talk to Maddux. To look at him and touch him and reassure herself that he really was okay before she did one of the most difficult things she'd ever had to do ... say goodbye and walk away from the one man she'd ever opened up her heart to.

She pressed a hand to the massive ache spreading throughout her chest, feeling as though a part of her was dying inside. The decision to leave Maddux was an incredibly painful one, because as much as she'd like to believe that she and Maddux Wilder could find their way to their own happily ever after, he'd never given her any indication that he wanted anything more from her than what they'd agreed upon the night of the ball. She'd given him her total surrender . . . and while it all should have just been a physical, sexual exchange, her heart and soul had gotten tangled up into the equation.

Beyond the brusque, callous man he'd been the evening they'd met, she'd managed to peel away enough layers to see a different side to Maddux. One who was kind and caring and gentler than she ever could have imagined. And so possessive and protective when it came to her. He'd like everyone to believe he was a gruff beast of a man, but somewhere along the way, he'd become her golden, shining prince.

She'd always known, from the very moment she'd offered herself for her father's debt, her time with Maddux had been marked as temporary, and now there was no longer any reason for their relationship to continue. He'd taken her out of revenge against a man who had destroyed his family, and tonight, Maddux's vengeance had been served and her purpose in his mission fulfilled.

Even if she and Maddux stood a glimmer of a chance at a future together, there was the bigger issue of all the bad blood between their families. Her father had killed his parents, and Hunter had made no secret of how much he despised her. As far as Maddux's brother was concerned, she was guilty by the sheer fact that she was Theodore's daughter. And after they'd lived for fourteen painful years with what her father had taken from their family, asking any of them to forgive and forget one of the most traumatic moments in their lives was something she'd never do.

"Ms. Cole?" a female voice called out, jarring Arabella out of her deep, agonizing thoughts.

Arabella glanced at the nurse. "Yes. That's me."

"You can see Mr. Wilder now." The other woman smiled at her. "He's in recovery while we process his discharge papers. I'll show you where he is."

Arabella followed the RN, and with every step she took closer to Maddux, her mind acknowledged what her heart refused to accept. . . that not all fairy tales ended happily ever after.

CHAPTER TWENTY-TWO

MADDUX SHIFTED IMPATIENTLY in the hospital bed he'd been assigned to as he waited to be released and to see Arabella. Over the course of the past few hours since being taken into the emergency room, he'd continually asked for her. But between having his laceration cleaned and stitched up and getting through the long, arduous process with the FBI agents who'd wanted his statement and being continually reminded by hospital staff that Arabella wasn't immediate family, he'd had to sit tight and deal with all the other bullshit first. Not an easy feat when he was a man who was used to getting what he wanted, right when he asked for it.

As soon as one of the nurses told Maddux she was going to get his discharge papers in order, he finally did the one thing he'd been dreading and called his sister. He'd opted for Tempest over Hunter since he'd been drinking earlier this evening, and quite frankly, Maddux wasn't in the mood to deal with his brother or the fact that he'd been the catalyst who'd put Arabella in harm's way. Maddux had calmly told Tempest he'd been in an accident—though he'd kept the details vague—and that he was at the hospital and was *fine*, but now needed a ride home. His car was still at the house where Gavin had taken Arabella, and Maddux would have one of his security guys go and pick it up later.

He'd heard the worry in his sister's voice, but she wasn't one to fall apart or have a meltdown. Tempest had always been strong and steady in the face of any kind of adversity, and she'd be grateful that Maddux was still alive, no matter the circumstances. That was Tempest... always seeing the positive in everything.

As for Hunter... Maddux wasn't sure what to expect of his brother these days, but as much as Maddux wasn't looking forward to the conversation to come, he needed to sit both his siblings down and tell them about the private, in-depth investigation he'd started years ago on Theodore, Gavin, and Addingwell Financial. He was certain they'd both be relieved to know that Theodore and Gavin were already behind bars and would likely remain there.

"He's right in here," Maddux heard a woman say, right before the RN led Arabella into his room. "It'll be about fifteen minutes before the paperwork is completed and he's discharged."

"Thank you," Arabella said softly, and as soon as she saw Maddux, a combination of relief and worry etched her beautiful features as she walked over to the side of his bed.

The skirt and blouse she'd worn to work that day were wrinkled and disheveled, her hair was tousled around her head, and she had dark smudges beneath her eyes. Her face was pale, and he hated that she'd had to endure the stress and scare of everything Gavin had put her through that evening. But she was alive, unharmed, and in one piece, and that's all Maddux cared about.

And because he did care about Arabella and only wanted the best for her, he knew he was going to have to let her go, no matter how much he wanted to keep her forever. But being the man responsible for putting her father away, probably for the rest of his life, was something he didn't think she'd ever forgive him for. In truth, she'd possibly grow to hate him or resent him, and could he really blame her when he'd been the one to destroy *her* life in one fell swoop?

He clenched his jaw. Honestly, the whole situation had been destined for heartbreak from the moment he'd agreed to take her in exchange for her father's debt. Maddux had wanted Arabella and all that sweet innocence, and because of his own selfish desires, he'd put her in a daunting situation a woman like her never should have been exposed to. It didn't matter that she'd found a way to make him smile more than he had in years. Or how he looked forward to watching her humorous antics or listening to her amusing dialogue through his security cameras. And mostly, how she made his soul feel lighter than it had since before his parents had died.

How funny was it that his greatest enemy's daughter had been the one to penetrate all those walls, tear down his emotional barriers, and make him crave everything with her? Love. Commitment. The possibility of a future.

Except she was never meant to be his. Their entwined pasts and fate had made certain of that.

"Hey," he said, his voice sounding and feeling like sandpaper in his throat as she stopped beside his bed.

"Hi, yourself." She smiled at him as she reached out and brushed his too long hair off his brow, her fingers gentle and cool against his warmer skin. "I just had to see for myself that you're okay."

"It's going to take more than a regular bullet to take me down," he teased, not wanting her to worry about him. "A few stitches and I'm good as new."

"Maddux . . . I want to thank you for risking your life for mine," she said as tears shimmered in her blue eyes and her bottom lip trembled. "And mostly, I'm so sorry that my father and Gavin were responsible for your parents' deaths. They both admitted to everything. How they were extorting money from them and other businesses and starting the grease fire in your parents' diner that ended up killing them both. Your hatred toward both of them is understandable. I can't even imagine the pain you and your brother and sister have gone through over the years, while my father and Gavin have continued to just live their lives as though nothing ever happened."

He groaned, hating the agony in her voice. And when she blinked and a few tears rolled down her cheeks, he lifted his good arm and tenderly wiped them away with his thumb. "Bella, you have nothing to apologize for. What happened wasn't your fault. You had no idea who your father worked for or what he did for a living."

"How could I have been so blind . . . to everything?" Her fingers skimmed down to his jaw, then lower, into the collar of his shirt, where she caressed the disfigured skin along his neck that he'd refused to talk about with her days ago. "These scars . . . were they caused by the fire that night? Gavin said you were there."

He wasn't sure what she'd been told by Gavin, but Maddux finally wanted to share that part of his past with her. Not because he wanted her to feel bad about what had happened but because, for the first time in his adult life, he knew he'd met a woman who truly cared. And she deserved to know the whole truth.

"Yes," he said, and forced himself to go back in time to that terrible night that changed everything for him and his siblings. "Your father and Gavin were extorting money from the small businesses in the area, and my parents were so tapped out financially from paying your father and

Gavin every month, while trying to support a family and pay their normal bills, and when my father finally put his foot down and told them he didn't have the money, they decided to make an example of my parents, so all the other businesses wouldn't revolt, too."

Arabella's fingers fell away from the side of his neck, and Maddux grabbed her hand, wanting that physical connection with her while he shared the most harrowing night of his life. "That night, after closing time, when my mother was in the back office doing paperwork, Gavin found a way into the diner and started the fire that blocked the way out of the office and the emergency exit, as well. My father and I were on our way back to the restaurant to pick up my mom when we saw the flames and the fire trucks arriving, and my dad didn't hesitate to run in to rescue my mom."

He swallowed hard as those awful, helpless emotions he'd kept buried for fourteen years threatened to break free. "The fire was so bad and spread so quickly, and I reacted on pure instinct when I pulled my father back out, then rushed in myself to save my mother, who I could hear screaming for help."

He shuddered at the horrific memories that still haunted his dreams and met her grief-stricken gaze. "But honestly, there was absolutely no way I could safely get to her. My shirt sleeve caught on fire just as a fireman dragged *me* out of the diner. The guy ripped my shirt off and snuffed out the spreading flames pretty quickly, or the burn would have been much, much worse. But that's when I saw my father lying lifelessly on the ground, being worked on by paramedics. He'd suffered a cardiac arrest, and no matter how hard or how long they tried to revive his heart, they just couldn't. I lost both of my parents that night."

A soft sob escaped from her lips, and the tears she shed on his behalf nearly shattered his heart. She leaned over and very gently hugged him, keeping all pressure off of his bad shoulder where the wound was. Her fingers slid through his hair, and she buried her face against his neck. "Maddux, I'm so sorry. I'd do anything to go back in time and change that day for you."

Tears stung his own eyes, and he gently smoothed his hand over the back of her head. "There is no changing the past, Bella. All I knew in that moment was that I was going to change the future," he said, needing to finish the story.

She straightened, her somber, understanding gaze looking in his. "Your revenge against my dad and Gavin."

He nodded. "Yes. My father told me about what Theodore and Gavin were doing prior to the blaze at the diner, and I knew it had to have been them who set the fire. So I found your father and confronted him, and while neither he nor Gavin ever admitted to setting the fire back then, your father told me point-blank that bad things happened when the protection fee wasn't paid, and that the other businesses needed to understand that there were consequences. I later found out that Theodore paid an official to cover up the fact that the fire was arson."

She shook her head, her expression pained. "God, that's not the father I knew. But knowing the true story, I can understand why you wanted to ruin him. He stole so much from you and Hunter and Tempest, and nothing can ever change that."

Yes, Theodore had stolen what mattered most to him and his siblings. And from that moment on, Maddux had vowed to one day bring down Theodore and Gavin. He'd become a bitter, coldhearted man outside of his brother and sister, his sole focus to amass as much fortune as possible so he could use that money and power to strip Theodore of everything that mattered the most to *him*.

And Maddux had finally succeeded . . . at the cost of devastating Arabella's life, too. And while there wasn't an ounce of bitterness or anger or hatred toward him in those soft blue eyes of hers right now, there was every chance that time would change all that. When everything finally sank in and she realized how ruthless he'd been in his quest to take down her father. The possibility that she'd one day come to hate him made his gut twist as sharp as a knife.

She suddenly worried her lower lip as she looked down at him, her brows furrowed.

"Tempest and Hunter... do they know what happened tonight?"

Arabella tried to pull her hand from his, and feeling her attempt to try and withdraw from him, Maddux tightened his hold, suddenly sensing that everything was about to change. "Not yet. After I watched you get pulled into the car off the street, my only thought was to get to you as quickly as possible, and I didn't have the chance to explain anything to either of them." Though he intended to. "My sister is on the way to the hospital to pick us up, and I'm sure she'll be bringing Hunter with her."

At the mention of his brother, Arabella stiffened, panic flashing across her features. "I need to go."

He frowned. "Go where?"

"Home. *My* home." She gave her hand a firmer tug, forcing him to release her. "There's no reason for me to go back to your place now that my father is in custody, and the last person your brother and sister are going to want to see right now is me, especially when they find out that you took a bullet to save my life. I'm sure Hunter will have a few choice things to say about that, which I'd rather not be around to hear."

"Fuck Hunter," he said on a low, furious growl, because he could feel her slipping through his fingers, even though he knew she'd never been his to begin with and this was always the way it would end between them—going their separate ways.

But still, his heart was beating so damn hard in his chest at the thought of losing her, and desperation suddenly gripped him. "Come home with me until we get everything figured out."

"There's nothing to figure out, Maddux." She took a step back, away from him, her expression heartbreakingly sad. "They're your family, and your loyalty is to them, not me. It never was, and it never will be, and that's okay," she said in a voice choked with emotion. "The truth is, there is just too much pain and heartache between our families, and I don't belong or fit into your or your siblings' lives."

He wanted to argue that she belonged *with him*, even though he knew *her* pain and heartache were a direct result of his act of revenge toward her father. Yeah, it was totally a fucked-up situation, but who knew that he'd fall hard for this woman who'd managed to thaw the ice around his heart in a very short time? "Bella—"

"I'm going," she said, cutting him off, the look in her eyes suddenly resolute. "Goodbye, Maddux."

She turned around, and with her shoulders straightening with pride, he watched her walk out of his hospital room . . . and his life.

CHAPTER TWENTY-THREE

NOTHING WAS THE same without Arabella. Maddux's apartment was too quiet and devoid of any warmth. His bed was too cold and filled with too many provocative memories of the two of them together intimately. And his heart . . . Jesus Christ, when had that organ become more than just a vessel to pump blood throughout his body? When did it develop the ability to ache for a woman he wanted so badly she consumed his thoughts twenty-four seven?

Standing out on his terrace, Maddux stared at the dark night sky and the twinkle of lights around the city. Up until a little over a week ago, everything he did had been fueled by rage and retribution, to the exception of anything else. He'd even taken Arabella as a form of revenge against her father, never imagining how one tiny, stubborn, and brave woman would change the way he viewed his life and his future.

Except without Arabella, his life and his future felt empty and bleak. And at the age of thirty-two, with so many years still stretching ahead of him, he felt as though an integral, emotional part of him was missing, thanks to the prospect of spending all that time alone and without her. He'd been so wrapped up in avenging his parents' deaths, and now that he'd accomplished his goal, there was nothing that gave him purpose anymore.

Sure, he had a billion-dollar tech and security company that he still needed to run, but he'd never been a man who felt as though he needed all the luxuries that money could buy when his main purpose for creating a small empire was to take care of his siblings and to build the capital to eventually take down Theodore Cole. Having money was nice, definitely, but all those tangible things he'd purchased over the years had never truly made him happy deep inside or fulfilled that hollow, isolated part of his soul . . . until Arabella.

What he now wanted more than anything was a reason for getting up in the morning and facing the day, knowing he actually had something to look forward to . . . like Arabella's sweet smiles. Her humor and the way she challenged him and aroused him and made him want to be a better man going forward in life.

Except a week had passed since she'd walked out of his hospital room, and he hadn't heard anything from her. Not that he'd expected to when she'd ended their short-lived relationship in a way that had finality written all over it. And things with him had been a little insane, too, with the takedown of Addingwell Financial, the dozens of arrests, and his involvement in the investigation.

He'd also had several meetings with his lawyer to transfer all of Theodore's assets into Arabella's name, which he'd yet to tell his siblings. Maddux had taken everything to hurt her father and cut the other man off at the knees, and he didn't want or need any of Theodore's property. Arabella, however, had nothing... and she deserved everything. He'd at least be able to give her what was rightfully hers to make her life a bit easier.

Inside his apartment, a chiming sound announced the arrival of the elevator on his floor. He turned around, leaned against the railing, and pushed his hands into the pockets of his slacks as he watched through the open French doors as his brother and sister walked into his place. His sister saw him out on the terrace first and headed in that direction, with Hunter following her, looking much more subdued and serious.

Something was definitely going on with his brother, but with Maddux's life in an upheaval since the night of the Wilder Way Charity Ball, he really hadn't had a chance to have a more personal conversation with Hunter to find out what had him so preoccupied, though he was guessing from what Tempest had told him, his brother's distracted mood had a lot to do with the woman who'd vanished on him the night after the ball. If that was the case, it was amusing to see him so twisted up over a female, when it had been years since he'd allowed one to get to him on anything deeper than a physical level.

Maddux exhaled a deep, heavy breath, because the conversation he was about to have with his siblings wasn't going to be an easy one. It was the one last issue he needed to resolve when it came to the whole Theodore situation, and there was no guessing how his brother and sister were going to react to what Maddux had decided.

His brother and sister now knew everything—from the years Maddux spent trying to build a case against Addingwell Financial and the front it had been for organized crime, which both Gavin and Theodore had been a part of, to Arabella being kidnapped by Gavin and the other man's intention to kill him, her, and Theodore. He'd sat them down the night of the shooting and told them the entire story, and while Tempest had been shocked and a little rattled by it all, Hunter had actually been contrite about his behavior toward Arabella that had sent her running in the first place.

But none of that changed the fact that Arabella was gone, and the two of their lives were entwined in such a way that they both believed they had valid reasons for keeping their distance. Because of Theodore killing his parents and Maddux being the one to finally incarcerate her father, they'd both believed their conflict was insurmountable. But the more he thought of the situation, and those emotionally driven arguments they were both clinging to, the more he realized that *nothing* was impossible. Maddux knew this lesson firsthand and had lived it his entire adult life.

When had he ever shied away from going after something he wanted, despite the obstacles in his way? Never. He'd never feared rejection, because he'd refused to accept that anything was beyond his reach or unattainable. It had never been in his nature to give up on anything worth having or admit defeat when it came to the important things that mattered the most to him . . . yet he'd given up on the one person who meant more to him than any possession he owned or any amount of wealth he'd acquired.

He'd let Arabella go when she'd needed him the most in her life. And God, the truth was, he needed her, too . . . in ways he never knew were possible. She was his other half, and without her in his life, his future was incomplete and would stay that way.

He wanted to give her everything . . . not because she'd lost her family and was completely alone, but because he loved her. The realization was a huge shock to his system. How the hell had *that* happened? He never believed falling in love was a possibility, but as the truth settled around him, he couldn't deny that Arabella fulfilled every part of him.

The epiphany hit him like a bolt of lightning, knocking sense into him as his brother and sister stepped out onto the terrace to join him. Jesus, what a fucking idiot he'd been for agreeing that Arabella walking away was for the best. It *wasn't* for the best. It was, quite possibly, the worst mistake he'd ever made.

"What's with that frown on your face?" Tempest asked, tipping her head at him curiously. "Is the discussion you asked us up here for that bad?"

"No." Maddux crossed his arms over his chest and shook his head. "I just realized what a dumb ass I am."

Hunter snickered. "You *just* realized that? I could have given you that news flash years ago."

Wanting to be civil, Maddux refrained, just barely, from flipping off his brother because he *had* set himself up for that reply.

A spark of optimism glimmered in Tempest's gaze. "Dare I hope that this dumb-ass revelation of yours has something to do with Arabella and the fact that you're miserable without her?"

Maddux grimaced at this sister's too accurate observation. "Is it that obvious?"

"To me, yes," she said with a soft, affectionate smile. "Only because I'm a woman and I noticed the changes in you while she was here. Despite everything with her father, you seemed incredibly fond of Arabella."

Maddux didn't want to get into his feelings about Arabella with either of his siblings, especially when it was becoming increasingly clear that being *fond* of Arabella was a very mild term for the emotions weaving in and around his heart. "Yes, my moment of clarity has to do with Arabella," he admitted, and was relieved when neither sibling, especially Hunter, balked at what Maddux was insinuating. "But before we get to that conversation, there's something I need to tell you both."

Tempest and Hunter looked at him expectantly, and Maddux forged ahead. "I went to my lawyer and had him transfer all of Theodore's assets to Arabella. I know I didn't run it by either of you, but the decision wasn't up for debate. The papers are done and just need to be delivered to Arabella for her signature, and then everything will be in her name, where it belongs." Maddux would be out three million dollars for paying off Theodore's debt, but that had been his choice, not Arabella's, and that money didn't matter to him. Arabella did.

His sister reached out and gently touched his arm. "It's the right thing to do," she said.

Hunter nodded solemnly. "I agree. She doesn't deserve to suffer for her father's offenses."

Relief swept through Maddux. He'd been unsure about Hunter's reaction, but it was clear that his brother was trying to make amends. "I'm taking the papers to Arabella tomorrow, and if I'm lucky, she'll be coming home with me. Permanently." He'd do everything in his power to persuade her to be his.

Always a romantic at heart, Tempest grinned happily and clasped her hands against her chest. "I knew this day would happen eventually. I knew some special woman would come along and chip away at all those hard edges you've built around your heart. And I'm so glad that woman is Arabella. She's soft and sweet where you're gruff, and you need calm and gentleness in your life. And I get the feeling she's not going to back down from your occasional surly attitude, either."

A grin tugged at the corner of Maddux's mouth. True, Arabella had already proven she could go toe to toe with him. The only time he wanted her submissive was in the bedroom, and so far that hadn't been an issue between them. No, his Bella loved surrendering her body and pleasure to him.

"Thank you," he said to his sister, and shifted his gaze to Hunter, wanting and needing his blessing, too.

Hunter exhaled a deep breath, his expression filled with sincerity. "I know she's nothing like her father, and if she makes you happy, then that's all that matters."

"She does," Maddux said, surprising himself with the spontaneous admission.

Tempest placed her hand on Maddux's cheek, looking into his eyes, searching for something, and seemingly finding it. "Yes, she *does* make you happy, and you deserve that, Maddy. You both do."

Maddux would have gone after Arabella regardless of his siblings' feelings, but he was incredibly grateful that he had their support, and that Arabella would be welcomed into their family and treated with respect.

He just prayed that his powers of persuasion were strong enough to convince his Bella that she belonged with him.

ARABELLA TAPED UP a box filled with her father's personal items and added the carton to the stack of others she'd been piling into the living room. Her dad had so much *stuff*, and with prison time looming in his future, it made the most sense to pack up things she thought he might want to keep and put them into a storage unit for now. She'd sell all the other unimportant but valuable items in the apartment and donate the rest.

It was an arduous, emotional process going through his personal effects, but it had to be done because she'd made the decision to move out of this too big and luxurious apartment she'd shared with her father in the city and would probably downsize to a cozy one-bedroom place near her work. This apartment belonged to Maddux, and considering what her father still owed him, he'd no doubt want to sell the place to offset the three-million-dollar debt he'd paid off, and she couldn't blame him for that.

After everything that had happened with Gavin and her father's arrest, Arabella had requested two weeks off from work to sort through her emotions, get her father's affairs in order considering the legal battle he was facing—though Arabella harbored no illusions that her dad wasn't guilty—and have the time to figure out the direction of her life and carve out her new normal, which she hadn't quite figured out yet.

She'd spent her days keeping her mind occupied with the to-do list she'd made, while at night she'd cried a lot of tears. For the things her father had done to hurt other people, for the loss of her only parent that now left her feeling alone in the world, and for the fact that she'd fallen in love with a man who held her heart and a piece of her soul . . . and she knew he always would.

At the thought of Maddux, her heart clenched in her chest, and she sat down on the nearest couch cushion, needing a moment before she dove back into all the packing again. There was no denying that she missed him, so much. More than she'd believed possible. There were so many times since that night at the hospital that she'd questioned her decision to walk away from him, and her reasons for doing so, when she knew they'd formed a strong, intimate bond in a very short time. But considering how quiet it had been, and she hadn't heard a word from him, she kept trying to convince herself she'd done the right thing. For both of them.

But had she? That was the question that haunted her. Confused her. Tangled up her heart and emotions and made her wonder if maybe, possibly, she'd given up much too soon on convincing Maddux that they might be able to take everything *good* about their time together and build a steady, permanent relationship from there based on creating happy, fun memories, that helped to ease the dark, painful past.

She wanted that for Maddux. She wanted it *with* Maddux. She didn't want them to end like a tragic fairy tale. She desperately wanted her happily ever after with him.

The doorbell rang, startling her out of her thoughts. She wasn't expecting company, and she stood up and grimaced as she glanced down at the dusty, faded jeans and plain T-shirt she was wearing. She'd run her fingers through her hair so many times in the past few hours, she knew it was probably a tousled mess, and she didn't have a lick of makeup on.

Not that she needed to impress anyone, she thought as she walked to the entryway, where she glanced out the peephole ... and gasped when she saw Maddux standing on the other side. Her heart raced with anticipation and hope. She couldn't imagine what he was doing here when everything between them had been silent for the past week, but she was curious enough to find out that she opened the door.

God, he looked so good. So gorgeous and golden and sexy, and it took restraint not to throw herself into his big, strong arms, just to feel him hold her again so she no longer felt so alone in the world.

"Hi," he said, his voice low and husky as his warm gaze roamed over her face, as if taking in every feature, every detail. "Can I come in?"

Her mouth had gone dry, and since speaking at the moment was difficult, she nodded and opened the door wider for him to enter, then shut it behind him. She led the way into the living room and turned around to find him frowning as he took in the dozens of boxes stacked everywhere before refocusing his attention on her.

"How are you?" he asked, tapping a dark yellow legal-sized envelope against his palm, the gesture almost . . . nervous.

"I'm okay," she replied, wondering how his gunshot wound was faring, which she'd thought about often since that night. "How's your shoulder?"

"Getting better." He gave her a tentative smile. "Still sore, but manageable."

"Good." She was glad to hear there hadn't been any permanent damage.

His gaze kept traveling back to the disarray in her living room and all the sealed cartons in the vicinity. When he finally looked directly at her again, she didn't miss the flicker of worry that passed across his features. "Are you going somewhere?"

"No . . . yes." The idle chitchat set her on edge, and she swallowed back the frustration rising to the surface. "Most of these boxes are my father's things, which I'm going to put into storage for now, but yes, I'll be moving soon to a smaller apartment so you can do whatever you want with this place. You can lease it or sell it. Whatever benefits you the most. I should be out in a month."

He was quiet, his expression intense, and that envelope still tapped away, increasing her own anxiety because it was difficult to stand right in front of the man of her dreams, knowing he was probably there to claim the property that was his, when all she wanted was *him*.

"Maddux . . . why are you here?" she flat-out asked him, needing to be put out of her misery already. Whatever he'd come there for, she'd give it to him, and then he could be on his way, and she could fall apart all over again once he was gone. Her heart was already tearing into shreds at the thought.

He exhaled a deep breath. "I wanted to deliver something to you, in person. *Two* things, actually," he amended, and extended the envelope toward her. "First, this."

She opened the flap and pulled out a sheaf of papers. Right on the front page, she caught the words "transfer of all listed assets to Arabella Cole," and beneath that, the complete list of all her father's possessions and property that had been signed over to Maddux a few days after he'd secured all of her dad's debt.

She shook her head in confusion. "What is this?"

He pushed his hands into the front pockets of his pants. "All your father's assets and property, it's all yours, Arabella. I'm giving it all back to you, and you can do whatever you want with all of it. It doesn't belong to me, it belongs to you."

Shock rippled through her as she blinked up at him. "What about the three million dollars you paid to clear my father's debt?"

A slight smile touched the corners of his mouth, and more than anything, she wanted to see it bloom into a full-fledged, sensual grin. "I'll write it off as a financial loss on my end. I don't want or expect anything in return."

The selfless gesture spoke to his character, but she would have given up everything all over again just to be with him. She knew that now her heart was on board . . . but was it too late?

Remembering he'd mentioned *two things* he was there for, she set the envelope and paperwork down on the coffee table and braced herself for the second part for his visit. "And the other thing you wanted to deliver?" she prompted.

"Oh, yeah, that . . . it's nonnegotiable."

She saw the steely determination in his gaze, witnessed the change in his demeanor that shifted his personality from kind and caring to pure alpha male in just a few beats. The word *nonnegotiable* meant whatever he wanted to ask her or give her or *whatever* was not up for discussion. She wasn't surprised that this assertive side to Maddux triggered a rush of heat to pour through her veins.

She licked her bottom lip, feeling as though things were taking a very seductive turn between them. "What is it?" she asked.

"A proposal," he said, drawing out the word so she couldn't mistake the sensual intent.

Wait . . . *what?* She thought about what he was asking, what he was *suggesting*, and she couldn't fight the disappointment when she figured out what he meant. "A proposal . . . as in, you want me to be your mistress?" Because she couldn't think of anything else he might want from her.

He shook his head, and with his fingers beneath her chin, he tipped her head back until her eyes locked on his. "No, not my mistress, Bella," he said, smiling. "A proposal . . . as in, I want you to be my lover. My fiancée. And someday, my wife. I know this is quick, but I don't want you to doubt for a second how much I want you and care about you and . . . I love you."

She sucked in a startled breath as those final three words came out of Maddux like they'd been locked away forever and were a little rusty. But Arabella knew this man well enough to know that he'd never say something he didn't mean. His declaration was not what she'd been expecting, but it was *everything* she could ever want or need in her life.

Emotion gathered in her throat, making it difficult to speak. "Maddux . . ."

"I know," he said, as if he understood what she was trying to express. "It shocked the hell out of me, too, but all I'm asking is that you give me a chance. That you give *us* a fighting chance."

Happy, hopeful tears were already rushing to her eyes. "Yes."

His expression softened at her words, his smile a wonder to behold. He framed her face in his palms, the gentle caress of his thumbs along her cheeks belying the strength in those big hands. "You are the first woman I've ever wanted to spend every single day with. We don't have to get married right away. We can have as long of an engagement as you like. I just need you to know how committed I am to you and that you mean *everything* to me."

His hands fell away for a moment as he withdrew a black velvet box from the front of his pants and opened the lid, causing her to gasp at the gorgeous ring he revealed—a perfect oval diamond surrounded by at least a dozen more brilliant stones.

"I want you to move in with me because I can't stand another fucking day in my apartment without you in it," he went on, blowing her away with this vulnerable side to a man who was always so controlled and held his emotions in check. "I want you to be the beauty that always calms the raging beast inside of me. You're the only one who can. Just say yes."

The word was on the tip of her tongue, but there was one thing holding her back from going all in. "What about your brother and your sister?"

"They gave me their blessing," he said with a huge smile that put all her fears to rest. "But even if they hadn't, I'd be here. Know that you come first for me, and always will, Bella. You've changed my life in so many ways. Let me spend the rest of our days together showing you what you mean to me, and the kind of future we can have together. I think it'll be pretty fucking awesome."

He was so sure of himself she couldn't contain the laughter that bubbled up out of her. "Yes, Maddux. I do love you, and yes, I want all those things, too."

He put the ring on her finger, and she squealed in pure joy and jumped up into his arms. His reflexes were sharp, and he easily caught her as she wrapped her legs around his waist, threaded her fingers through his hair, and kissed him with all the heat and depth and emotion rising inside her.

"Take me to my bedroom, please," she whispered against his lips as his hands cupped and squeezed her ass. "Down the hall, second door on the left. I want to consummate this engagement as soon as possible."

He groaned but didn't argue, and as soon as

they arrived in her room and he had her on the mattress, all their clothes came off in a mad rush to feel bare skin on skin. And then she was spreading her legs for him, making room for him in between. With a wicked grin, he lowered himself there and trailed hot, damp kisses up the inside of her thigh until his mouth covered her sensitive flesh and his lips and tongue and fingers had her trembling and moaning and coming beneath the onslaught of all that exquisite pleasure.

He moved up and over her, fitting his cock at her slick entrance, gradually pushing in and filling her until their bodies came completely together in one deep surge that had her crying out and clinging to him and Maddux shuddering with restraint.

He gave her a few seconds to catch her breath before he began moving in earnest, the friction of his thrusts driving them both back up to the peak, where they finally succumbed to the white-hot heat of passion waiting on the other side.

Once they both recovered, Maddux rolled to his back and gathered Arabella against his side. Content and overflowing with happiness, she snuggled against him and rested her head on his chest and slid one leg between his, entwining them intimately.

"You're coming home with me today, Bella," he said huskily, his tone brooking no argument. "And just for the record, I'm keeping you."

She smiled up at him. "For how long?"

"Forever," he promised, his arms tightening around her. "A lifetime. An eternity. Because now that you're mine, I'm never letting you go."

Arabella was okay with that. It really was hard to believe she'd wrapped her heart, soul, and life around his so quickly and completely, but the truth was, this man owned her. All of her. He had from that very first night when he'd taken her in exchange for her father's debt.

Their love story wasn't a conventional one, but for Arabella, the fairy tale was tangible and real.

And so was her happily ever after.

Don't miss, SINFUL PLEASURES, the next book in The Sinful Series featuring Hunter Wilder!

All Books in The Sinful Series:
Sinful Surrender
Sinful Pleasures
Sinful Proposition
Sinful Desires

Want more steamy-hot romance and deals? To stay up to date on Erika Wilde's latest releases, please sign-up for her newsletter here: erikawilde.com/subscribe

To learn more about Erika Wilde and her upcoming releases, you can visit her at the following places on the web:

Website:
erikawilde.com

Facebook:
facebook.com/groups/erikawildesfanclub

Instagram:
instagram.com/erikawilde1

Goodreads:
goodreads.com/erikawildeauthor

Printed in Great Britain
by Amazon